UNAUTHORIZED PASSION

AMANDA STEVENS

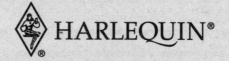

HARLEQUIN®

TORONTO • NEW YORK • LONDON
AMSTERDAM • PARIS • SYDNEY • HAMBURG
STOCKHOLM • ATHENS • TOKYO • MILAN • MADRID
PRAGUE • WARSAW • BUDAPEST • AUCKLAND

ISBN 0-373-22796-5

UNAUTHORIZED PASSION

This edition published by arrangement with Harlequin Books S.A.

® and TM are trademarks of the publisher. Trademarks indicated with ® are registered in the United States Patent and Trademark Office, the Canadian Trade Marks Office and in other countries.

www.eHarlequin.com

Printed in U.S.A.

ABOUT THE AUTHOR

Amanda Stevens is the bestselling author of over thirty novels of romantic suspense. In addition to being a Romance Writers of America RITA® Award finalist, she is also the recipient of awards in Career Achievement in Romantic/Mystery and Career Achievement in Romantic/Suspense from *Romantic Times* magazine. She currently resides in Texas. To find out more about past, present and future projects, please visit her Web site at www.amandastevens.com.

Books by Amanda Stevens

CAST OF CHARACTERS

Cassie Beaudreaux—Her innocent deception turns into a deadly charade.

Jack Fury—A former cop turned P.I., he vows to keep the glamorous actress safe. But can he trust himself with her?

Celeste Fortune—Is she in over her head or up to her neck in murder?

Max Tripp—Does he have an ulterior motive for putting Jack on Celeste's case?

Evelyn Ambrose-Pritchard—Cassie isn't the only guest at the exclusive Mirabelle Hotel with secrets.

Ethan Gold—Does the good professor have blood on his hands?

Olivia D'Arby—A second-rate actress with first-class ambitions.

Margo Fleming—A woman scorned.

Owen Fleming—His appetite for starlets could get him killed.

Lyle Lester—Does he have a thing for Celeste?

Danny Cantrell—He vows to get his bride back—no matter what it takes.

Chapter One

Jack Fury considered Dumpster-diving a metaphor for life—it could be unpredictable, messy and sometimes you just couldn't get the stink off no matter how hard you tried.

But he figured it was a necessary evil, kind of like sushi and cheap beer. You held your nose, dug in, and prayed to the real God that you wouldn't spend the rest of the night praying to the porcelain god.

He'd worshipped at that altar more times than he cared to remember, but considering the day he'd had—no, make that year—puking his guts out would be a fitting way to end it.

He stomped his feet in the rubber boots he'd pulled on, then surveyed the area once more before taking the plunge. It was a quiet Thursday night. He could hear traffic a few blocks over on Main Street, but in the alley behind the exclusive Mirabelle Hotel in Houston's Museum District, not a creature stirred.

Unless, of course, you counted the mosquitoes

and the giant flying cockroaches for which the Bayou City was famous. There were rats around, too, Jack suspected. Big, fat, urban-dwelling rodents that didn't skitter away at the sight of a human, but stared you right in the face and dared you, *dared* you, to enter their private domain.

Spraying himself down with heavy-duty insect repellent, he tossed the can back in his bag. Sweat trickled down his temples as he approached the dark blue trash bins. Even after dark, the temperature hovered around ninety and the humidity had a life of its own. There was no breeze to speak of, either. Some people considered August in Houston a little like hell on earth, but they were wrong. August in Houston was hell on earth to the third power. It was what the fiery depths of Hades only wished it could be.

This was Jack's city and he loved it.

The aroma wafting from the Dumpsters? Not so much. If there was anything he'd learned from his nearly ten years as a Houston cop it was that rich people's trash did, indeed, stink.

Smelled to high heaven, he thought as he bent over the first bin and began poking around with a stick. River Oaks, the Fourth Ward…didn't matter. Garbage was garbage. He hadn't minded the task so much when he'd still been a cop. Back then he would have happily crawled through a mountain of refuse to find evidence that would put away a killer or a clue that might help find a missing child. There'd been

times when he'd been so intent on the job at hand that he hadn't even noticed the smell.

Things were different now. Looking for receipts, letters, ticket stubs, anything that would give some rich techno geek the inside track on the hot babe he'd set his sights on was not exactly fulfilling work. It was downright distasteful, in fact. Little more than legal stalking, and as he sorted through the trash, Jack asked himself once more if he was really that desperate.

Overdrawn bank account? Check.

Final eviction notice? Check.

Furniture sold, car repossessed, stereo and TV pawned? Check, check and check.

Yep, he was that desperate.

His laptop was the only thing of value he had left, and he wasn't about to put that in hock. Without a computer he wouldn't be able to track the progress of the Casanova case, but then, if he didn't come up with something soon, there wasn't going to be any progress. As far as HPD was concerned, the case was closed. A suspect had been tried, convicted and was now serving consecutive life sentences in Huntsville for the brutal slaying of five women.

Jack had been one of the first detectives assigned to the task force tracking Casanova—a slick psycho who seduced his victims before killing them—and he'd been on the scene when the arrest had gone down. At first, he was as ecstatic as everyone else,

but then certain things had started to bother him. Not all the loose ends had been tied up by the arrest, and when word got out that he was still asking questions, he'd been kicked off the force for conducting an unauthorized investigation.

Just like that. No suspension, no review board, nothing. After ten years, he was out. Even the union had refused to help him because politics was politics. The mayor had agreed to back the union's demands in exchange for the police department's support of his Houston First initiative, an aggressive campaign strategy to give the city a higher profile. With an Olympic site committee coming to town, a serial killer on the loose didn't exactly fit with the image His Honor wanted to project.

Besides, the terror had finally come to an end, things were returning to normal and no one at city hall or HPD headquarters wanted a rogue cop stirring up trouble. So Jack was out.

But he wasn't finished with Casanova. Not by a long shot. He had a score to settle with a killer, and if in the meantime his own survival depended on getting the goods on some spoiled Hollywood starlet, then so be it.

"Her name is Celeste Fortune," his ex-partner, Max Tripp, had told him that first day when Jack had agreed to an interview. Max had left the police department five years earlier to open his own P.I. firm. He and Jack had eventually lost touch. Then out of

the blue, Max had called shortly after Jack had been fired. Max swore it was a coincidence, but Jack suspected that his ex-partner was still wired into the department, which was another reason he'd taken the job. If Max had contacts on the inside, Jack wanted them.

He'd also, by that time, spent so much of his own money on the Casanova investigation that he'd pretty much run out of options. Still, as Max had described the nature of his business that day, Jack had grown more and more uneasy.

"You want me to stalk this woman," he'd said incredulously. "Is that what I'm hearing?"

"No, of course, not." Max slid his hand down his silk tie. "I'm not asking you to do anything illegal. We're a legitimate business concern here."

"Yeah, well, sounds to me like you're walking a fine line," Jack muttered. "So maybe you'd better spell it all out just so there's no misunderstanding later on."

Max nodded. "Fine. I've nothing to hide. And I'm willing to do whatever it takes to get you on board. You're one of the best investigators I've ever worked with. We need a man with your talents around here, and if you play your cards right, you could be looking at a partnership down the road. Think about it, Jack. No more ground beef dinners. No more ten-year-old sedans that leave you stranded on the Southwest Freeway during rush hour." Max's critical gaze

swept over him. "I'll even give you an advance so you can get yourself some decent clothes and a good haircut."

Or pay his back rent. Designer duds, or a roof over his head? Tough call.

Max removed a folder from a drawer and placed it on top of the desk. "As I told you earlier, we have a very elite and discriminating clientele. The man who comes to us is more often than not a self-made millionaire, usually in the high tech field. He's in his thirties or forties, extremely intelligent, reasonably attractive and physically fit. He has all the accoutrements of wealth including investment portfolios, fast cars and beautiful homes in the most desirable locations. What he doesn't have is the perfect woman."

So who does? Jack wondered.

"But he's seen her. He knows who she is." Max stood and walked over to the bar to pour himself a drink. He offered one to Jack, but he declined. Scotch on an empty stomach? Asking for trouble.

Max came back to the desk and sat down. "Maybe he caught a glimpse of her getting into a cab. Or maybe their eyes met across a restaurant or their shoulders brushed on a crowded elevator. The point is, he knows she's the one. But so do dozens of other guys because this woman is something special. She has class, beauty, grace. Men flock to her in droves. Attractive, successful, very often wealthy men, not unlike our client. So how does he set himself apart

from the rest? How does he get her to single him out from the crowd? That's where we come in."

Max propped his feet on the desk and folded his hands behind his head. "We lay the groundwork for him. We talk to her friends, family, co-workers…anyone who can give us insight into her likes and dislikes. Her hopes and dreams. Her deepest, darkest secrets. We even look up old school chums and ex-boyfriends—all handled very discreetly, of course. We find out her favorite books, her favorite restaurant, the kind of music she listens to. Then, when we have everything we need, we design a coincidental meeting between her and the client. We arrange for them to be seated next to each other at an Astros game…or at the Wortham Center, depending on her tastes. We arm our client with the right information to arouse her interest, ignite that initial spark and then…the rest is up to him. And nature."

"It's dishonest," Jack said flatly. "It may not be illegal, what you're doing, but it sure as hell ain't ethical."

Max picked up his drink. "Think of it this way. If these two are meant to be together, all we're really doing is giving fate a little nudge. But if it doesn't work out, they go their separate ways. She never has to see him again. No harm, no foul."

"But what if she does want to see him again? What if she falls for him?" Jack argued. "He's selling her a bill of goods by pretending to be something he's not."

"Are you telling me you've never pretended to be

interested in something just to get a woman's attention?" Max gestured with his glass. "Say you meet
her in a bar. You get to talking. She mentions a movie
she just saw and loved. You saw the same movie and
hated it. But this woman…she's hot, you know?
Someone you'd definitely like to hook up with. Do
you admit you're not into chick flicks and risk turning her off, or do you lie and say you like any film
with Tom Hanks just to keep the conversation
going?"

Jack scowled. "That's different."

"Yes, it is," Max agreed. "Because this woman
you meet in the bar…you're not looking for anything
more serious than a good time. No commitment. Just
a casual relationship. Maybe even just a one-night
stand. But our client is looking for the woman of his
dreams. Someone with whom he can share his life—
and his money, I might add. Given all that, some
might say we're doing the woman a favor."

Jack still wasn't convinced, but did he really have
a choice here? Offers hadn't exactly come pouring
in since he'd gotten the boot from the police department. In the meantime, Casanova was still out there
somewhere. Without funds, Jack had no way to find
him and stop him before he killed again. And he
would kill again. It was only a matter of time.

He ran his hand through his hair. "Tell me more
about the target."

With one finger, Max shoved the folder across the

desk. "Take a look for yourself. There's a picture of her inside."

Reluctantly, Jack opened the folder and removed the eight-by-ten glossy. As he studied the photograph—obviously a professional headshot—something prickled along his backbone. Not nerves or even a lingering distaste over what he'd been reduced to. No, his reaction was purely visceral, a physical response to the woman's blatant sexuality. She practically oozed sex, from her tousled blond hair to her heavy-lidded blue eyes and her full lips that were glossed and parted and looking as if they were made to—

"Jack?"

He glanced up.

Max grinned. "She's something, isn't she? Do you recognize her?"

"Can't say that I do." Jack returned his gaze to the picture. "Is there some reason I should?"

"She's been in a few movies, done some TV spots. She's still relatively obscure, but her last few roles have won her a fair amount of critical acclaim and she seemed on the verge of breaking out before she became embroiled in a scandal that pretty much stopped her career dead in its tracks."

"What kind of scandal?" Jack's curiosity was piqued in spite of himself.

"She was involved with some big shot producer by the name of Owen Fleming out in L.A. Ever heard of him?"

Jack shook his head. He didn't pay much attention to movies unless he wanted to impress a woman. Which kind of made Max's earlier point, he supposed.

"They managed to keep the affair under wraps for several months," Max said. "Then he bought her this huge diamond which she flashed around L.A., and the wife got wind of it. The whole thing blew up into a nasty PR mess, and apparently Celeste decided to get out of town until things cooled off. We figure that's why she's back in Houston."

"What do you mean she's *back* in Houston?"

"She went to school here. From what I understand, she's still pretty tight with her old drama professor at the university. They even lived together for a while before she took off for L.A. You may want to talk to him at some point as well as to her current roommate." Max reached for the folder and flipped through the pages. "Olivia D'Arby. She's an actress, too, although her parts seem to be few and far between."

"What about the client? Who is he?" Who was the guy willing to plunk down $75,000—and that was just for starters—for a "chance" encounter with Celeste Fortune?

"I can't tell you that. The identity of our clients remains confidential, even to our operatives." Max took another sip of his scotch. "So…what do you say? Are you in?"

Yeah, he was in. But after a week on the job, Jack was more certain than ever that he didn't have the stomach for this kind of work. He hated to think that he might actually be giving off the same sleazy, stalker vibe as some of the low rent P.I.s who used to hang around the police department, hoping to pick up a tip.

He had to admit, however, that it was easy money. Most people would probably be amazed by the amount of their personal information that could be accessed with little more than a phone call or a Google search.

Celeste Fortune was no exception. Since Jack had taken the assignment, he'd learned all kinds of interesting tidbits about her, but the broader picture was that of a small-town girl searching for love—and fame—in all the wrong places.

The story was as old as Tinseltown itself, and as Jack finished with the first Dumpster, he wondered again why a woman with Celeste Fortune's looks and talent had allowed herself to become such a cliché.

And now another man wanted her. Another man was willing to pay a small fortune to have her.

But in the week since he'd started watching her, it was Jack who had unwittingly fallen under her spell.

SHE STOOD in front of the full-length mirror in the bedroom of her suite, her gaze going from her reflec-

tion to the magazine cover that she'd propped on the nearby dresser. She sighed. Who was she trying to kid? There was no way she could measure up to that airbrushed fantasy. She must have been out of her mind to think that she could ever be anything more than a small-town girl with big dreams and a penchant for trouble.

Just look at the mess she'd made of things, and she was only twenty-eight. There was no telling how screwed up her life would be by the time she turned thirty. And it wasn't like running away was going to resolve the situation. If anything, it would only prolong the agony.

Still, leaving had seemed like a good idea at the time. "If you can't stand the heat, get out of the kitchen," her mother had always advised, and taking that counsel to heart, she'd fled town in the middle of the night, and now here she was, holed up in a ritzy boutique hotel in Houston.

Going stir-crazy.

Honestly, what good did it do to be in the city of her dreams, trying to start a new life, if she couldn't even leave her suite? Would it really hurt to take a brisk walk through Hermann Park or a leisurely stroll along Montrose Boulevard? What would be the harm in visiting a museum or two, or having lunch at one of the trendy eateries on restaurant row?

She'd had her heart set on taking in all those

places until her cousin, Sissy, had firmly disabused her of the notion.

Sissy Fontenot aka Celeste Fortune.

"All the stars use look-alikes nowadays when they want to avoid the press," her cousin had explained on the phone a few days ago. "So when my publicist suggested I get a decoy until this mess blows over, I immediately thought of you, Cassie. Remember how people always used to think we were twins when we were little?"

"Well, we are double cousins," Cassie murmured, still flabbergasted by Celeste's proposition. Could she, Cassie Boudreaux, really pretend to be a glamorous movie actress? Could she pull it off? Did she dare even try?

What a question. Of course she dared if it meant getting out of Manville, Louisiana, and away from the hateful glances—not to mention voodoo hexes—of the Cantrell clan. Leaving their golden boy at the altar hadn't exactly endeared Cassie to Danny's family.

"I haven't seen you in years," Celeste said carefully. "You haven't…put on a lot of weight or anything, have you?"

Cassie sent up a quick prayer of thanks for the fifteen pounds she'd lost since her breakup with Danny. "Uh, no. I'm still the same size I was in high school." More or less.

"Are you sure? Because I happened to see your

engagement picture in the *Manville Gazette*, and I thought—now don't take this the wrong way—I thought you might be starting to take a little after Grandma Boudreaux."

Cassie tried to control her outrage. She did *not* take after that evil old woman in any way, shape or form. Not only had their grandmother possessed a nasty disposition, she'd weighed well over three hundred pounds at the time of her death. The family had had to choose her pallbearers accordingly.

"That picture was shot from a bad angle," Cassie insisted. "And besides, the camera adds ten pounds."

"I took that into consideration," Celeste blithely informed her. "Anyway, I was surprised by how much you still resemble me. In the face, I mean. You'll need to lighten your hair, of course, but for God's sake, don't get it done down there." Cassie could picture her cousin's shudder. "I'll make arrangements with a salon in Houston. They'll do your nails, too, and show you how to wear your makeup. Oh, and start working out, okay? From what I could see in that picture, you could stand to firm up a little, and it's never too late to start counting the old calories. We've still got a few days. If you watch your carbs, you could drop ten pounds before we meet in Houston."

Drop ten pounds? In a matter of days? Maybe in Dreamworld, Cassie thought acerbically. But in the real world it had taken a major life crisis to fi-

nally pry off the freshman fifteen she'd been carrying around since college. And as for exercise, she'd had to give up her daily walks after Earl Cantrell, Danny's uncle, had tried to run her over one morning.

"Don't expect me to go on some starvation diet just so I can fit into your size zeros," Cassie said resentfully. "I like the way I look."

"And I'm sure you look just fine." *For you,* Celeste's tone implied. "Look, it'll hardly matter. After everything that's happened, who would be surprised if I'm not looking my best? And besides, no one will get more than a glimpse of you anyway. You won't be leaving the hotel except when you take Mr. Bogart for his walks."

"Mr. Bogart?"

"My Chihuahua. I hate leaving him behind, but it might look strange if you were spotted without him. He goes everywhere with me. Don't you, sweetie?"

Cassie heard what sounded like a whimper on the other end, then her cousin said anxiously, "You'll take good care of him, won't you? He likes to go out first thing in the morning and right before he retires in the evening. And he has to eat three meals a day or his little system gets all out of whack."

"Don't worry," Cassie said with a grimace. "I'll treat him like he was my own." Which wasn't saying much considering she really wasn't a dog person. "Look, Sissy—"

"Celeste."

"Look, Celeste, are you saying the only time I can leave the hotel is when I take the dog for a walk? I mean, we're talking a whole month here."

"A whole month in a luxury hotel. You'll have your own Jacuzzi and steam shower, not to mention twenty-four-hour room service."

"I know, but a whole month?" Now it was Cassie who shuddered.

Celeste sighed. "I guess you're right. I guess that is too much to ask, even of family."

Even as a child, her cousin had been an expert travel agent when it came to guilt trips, but this time Cassie wasn't booking.

When she said nothing, Celeste gave another dramatic sigh. "Okay, tell you what. I'll plan a few outings for you in advance. I'll even make all the arrangements. That way, if any of the paparazzi should somehow find out where you're staying—I mean, where *I'm* staying—a glimpse of you—me— now and then might help convince them that I'm flying solo these days."

In other words, no Owen Fleming.

"Where will you be?" Cassie couldn't help asking, although she already had her suspicions. Why would Celeste go to so much trouble, not to mention expense, to set up such an elaborate ruse if she wasn't planning an assignation with her married lover?

"Don't you worry about that. You just concentrate

on convincing everyone that Celeste Fortune is in seclusion nursing a broken heart."

Her cousin's evasive answer did little to assuage
Cassie's qualms. If Margo Fleming got wind of a
tryst between her husband and Celeste, there'd be
hell to pay. It could literally cost Owen a fortune and
Celeste, what was left of her career.

From everything Cassie had read of the scandal—
and she'd devoured every juicy morsel she could get
her hands on—Margo Fleming was a powerful
woman in the film industry. She'd bankrolled
Owen's first few productions, and she could make or
break a budding starlet.

Her cousin was playing with fire. But then, that
was the Boudreaux way, wasn't it?

JACK HAD JUST finished going through the last Dumpster when a noise alerted him that he was no longer
alone in the alley. It was a subtle sound, kind of like
a whimper. He might have chalked it up to the rodents skulking about nearby except…he'd never
known a rat to snivel.

Nor had he ever seen one dragging a leash, he
thought, as he watched the tiny creature ease toward him through the shadows. When the Chihuahua was close enough, Jack knelt down and put
out his hand. The dog hesitated, then came pranc-
ing over.

"Are you lost?" Jack reached for the collar,

then jerked back when the Chihuahua snapped at his hand.

Slowly he stood. "Okay, okay, no touching. I get it."

A woman's voice called from the street, "Mr. Bogart? Where the he—where are you, sweetie? Come to Mother."

Jack glanced down at the dog. "Sounds like you're being paged. Be a good boy and run along."

The Chihuahua stared at him unblinkingly and began to wag his tail.

"Oh, so now we're friends, all of a sudden?"

"Mr. Bogart? Are you down there?" The woman was in the alley now, her voice getting more frantic by the moment. Any second now she would come around the corner, spot Jack, and then would undoubtedly alert the night manager of a prowler, who in turn would probably call the police. And since there was no good explanation for Jack's presence behind the Mirabelle at that time of night, he decided it would be best all around to avoid such a confrontation.

He tried to quietly shoo the dog away by waving his hand. When that didn't work, he whispered fiercely, "Go! Vamoose! Am-scray!" The tail wagged even harder, and Jack could have sworn the damn dog grinned at him.

Muttering an oath, he moved out of sight behind one of the Dumpsters just as the woman came hurrying around the corner.

"Mr. Bogart! Come on, now. It's not funny anymore. If you-know-who finds out—" The woman stopped short when she saw the dog. "Mr. Bogart?"

The dog didn't move. His beady gaze remained fixated on Jack.

"What's the matter with you?" The woman's voice lowered. "What do you see behind there?"

If she came any closer, she would spy him, Jack thought. He glanced at the dog. "Get lost," he mouthed.

Obviously not one to take a hint, the Chihuahua ran over, lifted his leg, and peed on Jack's boot.

"…the hell!" Jack jerked his foot reflexively, and the dog, disturbed in the middle of a call from nature, began to yap at the top of his little lungs.

The woman gasped when she saw Jack.

And Jack froze. His breath rushed out of his lungs, and he felt tingles all up and down his spine. There she stood, the object of his fascination, mere inches away. So close he could reach out and touch that honey-gold skin of hers, stroke his hand down her sexy blond hair, which was now covered by a scarf. She wore dark glasses, too, even though it was night, but Jack would have known her anywhere….

For the longest moment, no one but the dog said anything.

Then Celeste Fortune came at him so fast Jack barely had time to react. "What the hell do you think you're doing, you pervert? What kind of monster kicks a defenseless little dog like that?"

Jack managed to put up an arm to ward off the first blow.

"Help! Police!" she screamed.

As she drew back to swing her purse again, Jack took that as his cue to get the hell out of there. He picked up his bag and sprinted—as best he could in rubber boots—down the alley.

Celeste Fortune's shrieks followed him all the way to the street, and as he hurried toward his borrowed car, he heard the wail of a police siren a few blocks over.

Man, she was *good*.

"...POLICE AT THIS HOUR are on the scene of a brutal homicide in the Montrose area. Very little information is being released to the public, but we have learned that the victim was a young woman in her late twenties, and neighbors say she lived alone. The similarities to the five grisly murders that occurred here last summer are bound to stir a lot of bad memories for residents in this area. As the viewers will recall, John Allen Stiles, also known as the Casanova Killer, was convicted on five counts of first-degree murder and is now serving consecutive life sentences at Huntsville. But there are some who still maintain his innocence, including a former HPD detective."

With a shiver, Cassie turned off the TV. She didn't want to be reminded of those murders. Even in her little hometown, the brutality of the killings had sent

shock waves through the community, and people who had never locked their doors before were suddenly installing dead bolts and leaving porch lights on all night.

Cassie fit the profile of the killer's victims. She was young, single and she lived alone. But she hadn't gotten caught up in the panic because Houston had seemed a long way off to her then. But now here she was...and another killer was apparently on the loose...

A chill raced up her spine at the sound of yet another siren. Across the room, Mr. Bogart stirred restlessly in his bed, then rolled over and went right back to sleep. Sated from gourmet treats, he seemed none the worse for their earlier adventure.

Cassie couldn't say the same for herself. She still didn't know what had possessed her to attack that man in the alley except—even though she was no dog person—she'd never been able to stand animals of any kind being mistreated. And when she'd seen him kick Bogey like that, her reaction had been instinctive.

"Pervert," she muttered. But what if the guy was worse than that? What if he was the one who had killed that poor woman tonight? Should she call the police?

And tell them what?

She hadn't gotten a good look at the man's face, nor did she know which direction he'd fled after he

left the alley. A call to the police would accomplish nothing more than to blow her cover. And Celeste's.

And, anyway, he was probably just some homeless guy going through the Dumpsters.

But…what if he wasn't?

The sirens grew louder, and reluctantly, Cassie walked over and opened the French doors. Stepping outside, she glanced around. The secluded balcony overlooked a quiet tree-lined street. It reminded her of a Parisian boulevard she'd once seen in a picture.

The small, exclusive hotel was only three stories, and in August, it operated at less than half capacity. When Celeste had made the reservations, she'd had her choice of suites. She'd put Cassie on the third floor, at the far southeast corner where she not only had a view of the street, but also of the narrow alley that provided access to the service entry of the hotel.

The siren sounded as if it was only a block or two from the rear of the hotel, and as Cassie peered over the balcony into the shadows, she spotted someone moving about below her. A tall figure dressed in black…

Casanova!

She instantly chided herself for letting her imagination get the better of her. Hadn't she just heard on the news that John Allen Stiles was still serving time in Huntsville?

But there were some who believed in his innocence. And another woman had been murdered just

a few blocks from where Cassie stood. What if that police detective was right? What if the real Casanova was still out there somewhere? What if she'd come face-to-face with him earlier?

Below, the figure moved out of the shadows and was caught for one brief moment in a glimmer of light from the street. As he turned his head toward the balcony, Cassie caught her breath.

She *knew* him.

Chapter Two

Jack tried to let himself into his apartment as quietly as he could, but before he could get inside the door across the hall opened, and his neighbor, Cher Maynard, popped her head out.

"I've been waiting for you," she said in that low, husky voice of hers. The woman could read a phone book and make it sound pornographic.

Jack winced, then plastered a smile on his face as he turned. "Yeah? I figured you'd given up on me by now."

Her gaze slipped over him. "On you? Never."

He walked over and handed her a set of keys. "Thanks for the use of your car, by the way. You're a lifesaver."

"I didn't exactly do it out of the goodness of my heart, now did I? We have a deal, remember? I scratch your back…you scratch mine." She stepped back and motioned with her head for him to join her in her apartment.

Jack hesitated, trying to buy himself some time. "Are you sure? It's late. Maybe we should do this some other time—"

"Oh no you don't." She curled a hand around his arm and yanked him inside the apartment, then slammed the door with her foot. Reaching behind her, she turned the dead bolt.

"Look, Cher, it's been a long day. I'm wiped. If I could just crash for a few hours"

"Now, Jackie, don't you worry." Her smile worried him a great deal. "I'll do all the work. All you have to do is relax and enjoy."

Easier said than done, Jack thought as he glanced warily around her apartment. The one-bedroom unit was a veritable treasure trove of garage sale and secondhand finds. The red silk pillows and beaded lamp shades were charming, eccentric and a little overpowering, not unlike the woman who lived there.

His gaze moved back to Cher. They'd been neighbors for nearly two years, but her appearance still provoked a double take now and then. Her dark, glossy hair hung to her waist, and her eyes were heavily lined to resemble the seventies version of her famous namesake. She favored rhinestone-studded jeans, cropped tops and four-inch stilettos that put her just a smidgen over Jack's six feet.

He'd never been sure which had come first, the name or the look. She'd told him once after a few too many margaritas that her real name was Char-

lene. He couldn't exactly remember what he'd told her that night.

She walked over now and ran a long, tapered nail down the front of his shirt. "You might want to take that off. Things are apt to get a little messy before we're through."

"It's chilly in here," he said nervously. "I think I'll leave it on if you don't mind."

She slanted him a look through her false lashes. "What's the matter, Jackie? You're not getting cold feet, are you? It's not like we haven't done this before."

She pushed him toward the old, flea market barber's chair that she'd pulled up next to the kitchen sink. "Have a seat and we'll get started. Are you sure you don't want to remove your shirt?"

He sank into the chair and sighed. "Let's just get this over with."

"Just what every girl wants to hear." She whipped out a plastic cape and gave it a good snap.

"So…what exactly are you planning to do?" Jack eyed the bottles and mixing bowls on the counter beside the sink.

Cher tied the cape around him, then patted his shoulder. "All you need to know is that you're in good hands."

"Famous last words," he muttered.

"No grumbling. We had a deal, remember? I lend you my car and in return, I get to practice on your hair until I graduate from beauty school."

Which couldn't come soon enough for Jack. He'd had four haircuts in a three-week span. At this rate, he'd be bald by the time Cher got her diploma.

"Look at you. You're all knotted up." She began to massage his shoulders and the back of his neck. "I bet all this tension has something to do with that murder in Montrose earlier tonight. When I heard about it on the news, I immediately thought of you and what you always say about Casanova—that he's still out there somewhere. Jackie…you don't think it was him tonight, do you?"

"I don't know," Jack admitted. He hadn't been able to get much from his contacts at HPD. For whatever reason, the brass was keeping a tight lid on the flow of information about the latest homicide. Which made Jack all the more suspicious. Were they trying to cover up a connection to Casanova?

Cher shuddered. "Let's talk about something else. It gives me the creeps just thinking about that monster roaming around out there." Her knuckles kneaded Jack's shoulders. "So tell me about your day. Are you still following that actress around?"

He frowned. "I'm not exactly following her around. She never leaves the hotel." Until tonight. Tonight, he'd seen her up close and personal, and the meeting had left him oddly unsettled. Maybe it was because he'd bought in to her Hollywood image, had begun to think of her as some celluloid goddess, and then seeing her in person had made him realize that

she was a real flesh-and-blood woman. She could be hurt by what he was doing.

Cher's fingers continued to work their magic, and he sighed as the tension finally began to seep away.

"Hey, Jack?"

The massage was so relaxing, he'd almost drifted off. "Yeah?"

"What else have you learned about Celeste Fortune?"

"You know I don't like to talk about my work." It had been a mistake to say anything to Cher about the assignment. He hadn't meant to, but she'd overheard him on the phone with Max the other day, and since he'd needed to borrow her car, he couldn't exactly tell her to kiss off when she started asking questions.

Besides, he also didn't want her to think—and blab around the complex—that he was some freak who kept pictures of a relatively obscure actress in his apartment.

"Come on. Don't be so coy." Cher's hands moved back to his neck, and she deepened the massage. *"Just admit it, why don't you? You have a little crush on her."*

"That's crazy."

"No, what's crazy is that you think she won't be pissed when she finds out what you're doing. Besides, a woman like her is way out of your league, Jackie."

"I realize that. But I don't have a crush on her, anyway. Boys get crushes. Men get—"

"Obsessions? First Casanova and now Celeste Fortune. Anyone ever tell you you're a little on the neurotic side?" Cher plowed a knuckle into a knot at the back of Jack's neck and he jumped.

"Ouch! Anyone ever tell you you're a little on the sadistic side?"

"Oh, shut up and take it," she muttered. "You deserve it."

"What the hell did I do?"

"You're a man."

So that was it. The latest Mr. Right had evidently turned out to be another dud. At least by Cher's standards. Jack wondered what had been the matter with this one. The previous guy had parted his hair on the wrong side, and the one before that had preferred boxers instead of briefs. Or briefs instead of boxers. Jack couldn't keep up. The point was, Cher was picky when it came to romance.

But her love life was something she'd have to sort out on her own. Jack had his own problems. Slumping down in the chair, he closed his eyes and thought about Celeste Fortune.

"Just admit it, why don't you? You have a little crush on her."

Was he that obvious?

The stack of videos in his apartment had probably been the giveaway.

How could a woman as beautiful and glamorous as Celeste Fortune allow herself to get mixed up

with a sleaze like Owen Fleming? The man was a typical Hollywood player, from what Jack had been able to find out. He'd married a rich wife, then proceeded to go through starlets like a pig at a feeding trough.

Jack thought about the way Celeste had come at him tonight, all fired up, blue eyes undoubtedly blazing behind those dark glasses. He had a feeling she'd be a real pistol in bed, but it wasn't likely he'd ever find that out. However, that didn't stop him from fantasizing, and he let himself conjure up all sorts of interesting scenarios as Cher worked on his hair.

An hour and a half later, she removed the cape and tossed it aside. "All done. That wasn't so bad, was it?"

Jack stretched. "Guess not. I think I must have dozed off a few times." He put a hand to his hair. "Feels short."

"Hardly more than a trim."

"Really? So what was all that smelly gunk you put on my head?"

"Oh, just a deep, penetrating conditioner."

"A conditioner, huh? Well, it burned like hell. Let me see that mirror—"

When he reached for the hand mirror on the counter, Cher grabbed it and put it behind her back. "You don't trust me?"

"I want to see for myself." When Jack reached for the mirror again, she took a step back.

"It's late," she said in a rush. "I think you should just sleep on it, and then when you wake up in the morning, you'll be all refreshed and ready to face the world with your brand-new…look."

Jack's gaze narrowed. "What do you mean, my new look? What the hell did you do?"

"Nothing. It may be a little…shorter than we talked about. Now don't freak," she hastened to add when he grabbed the mirror from her. "It'll just take some getting used to, that's all."

"Ho…ly…sh—"

"Oh, come on. It's not that bad."

"Compared to what?" Jack turned his head first one way, then the other. It was short all right. Short and…blond. Bleached blond. What little hair he had left was now the color of straw. And it appeared to have roughly the same texture. "Fix it, Cher. I can't walk around like this."

Cher assumed a wounded expression. "Fix it? Why would you want to fix it? The color looks great on you."

Jack sighed. "In other words, you can't."

"We haven't gotten to that part yet," she admitted sheepishly. "But if you can get past the shock, I think you'll like it. You might even thank me for it later. The color really does show off those gorgeous eyes of yours and those dreamy cheekbones. Not to mention your tan. If nothing else, it'll make you stand out in a crowd."

"In my line of work, that's hardly a plus." Jack glanced in the mirror again. Okay, maybe Cher was right. Maybe it wasn't that bad. Maybe it wasn't quite as short or as blond as he'd first thought. And the color did set off his eyes...

"Do me a favor," she said. "Just give it a day or two. If you still don't like it, you can come down to the beauty school and I'll have my instructor take a look at it—"

The phone interrupted her and Cher glanced at her watch. "Oh, no. I had no idea it was so late."

Jack's brows shot up at her nervousness. "What's the matter? Got a hot date?"

"Uh, no. That's probably just my mother calling."

"At this hour?"

"She sometimes loses track of time. You know how it is with old people."

Jack had met Cher's mother. The woman wasn't a day over fifty, and she had a body that wouldn't quit. "Aren't you going to answer it?"

"She'll call back. She always does." Cher grabbed his arm, pulled him from the chair, and began to hustle him toward the door.

Jack turned. "About your car—"

"Oh, yeah, sure, you can use it tomorrow. I've still got my brother's car. I can take that to class." She grabbed her keys from the table and all but threw them at him. Then she opened the door and gave him a shove.

Jack stubbornly resisted. "Hey, what gives? If I didn't know better, I'd think you're trying to get rid of me."

"It's late, that's all, and I'm tired—"

Behind her, the answering machine picked up and Cher's recorded greeting—a really bad rendition of "I've Got You Babe"—began to play.

Jack wanted to wait around to hear the message, but Cher was having none of that. With a quick "Good night," she slammed the door in his face, and he was left standing in the hall, wondering why that phone call had flustered her so much.

CHER CAST an uneasy glance toward the door as she lowered her voice. "I told you I'd be in touch when I have something."

She listened for a moment, her hand clutching the phone as the caller's tone grew more belligerent. "Calm down. I know ten thousand dollars is a lot of money. I know we have a deal. I'm trying to hold up my end, but you've got to give me some time."

Another pause, then Cher said shakily, "Look, there's no call for threats—"

But the line had gone dead, and as Cher hung up the phone, she felt the first tremor of fear at what she'd done.

CASSIE COULDN'T SLEEP. She couldn't get her mind off the man she'd seen looking up at her balcony. She

knew him. Knew his face, but she couldn't place him. It was maddening, that glimmer of recognition, then nothing more.

Was he the same man she'd seen earlier in the alley?

Was he the killer?

But according to the news, the murder had taken place hours ago. Why would the killer still be lurking in the area? Wouldn't he want to put distance between himself and the crime scene?

Unless he was afraid of being spotted on the street. Or unless...he lived nearby.

Finally, Cassie had worked herself up into such a state that she'd put back on the scarf and dark glasses, left the hotel, and gone across the street to use the pay phone she'd spotted earlier. When the operator had answered, she'd asked to speak to the detective in charge of the murder investigation, and to her surprise, she'd been put right through.

But the officer she'd spoken to sounded too young to be a detective, and rather than heading up a homicide investigation, Cassie suspected he'd been assigned the unenviable task of fielding all the crank calls that had undoubtedly come pouring in after the news broadcast.

He had politely taken down all her information, but he hadn't seemed to attach much significance to what she'd seen. Maybe it was because they'd already apprehended a suspect, Cassie thought hopefully. Or maybe eyewitnesses at the scene had given

an entirely different description of the killer. Whatever the cause for the officer's cavalier attitude, Cassie was just glad she'd done her civic duty. Now she could go to bed with a clear conscience and get a good night's sleep.

But now, in addition to worrying about whether or not she'd come face-to-face with a killer, she had to wonder if the police would be able to somehow trace that call back to her. She hadn't given her name, or Celeste's, but her voice had undoubtedly been taped. What if they came around the hotel asking questions? Should she continue to pretend to be Celeste, or should she come clean and give them her real name?

And if she did come clean, what would Celeste say?

And more important, what would Margo Fleming do if she found out what Celeste was up to?

Not your problem, a little voice reminded her. If Celeste had taken up again with her married lover, that was her business, but a tawdry affair couldn't be allowed to take priority over a murder investigation.

Perhaps the best thing Cassie could do to truly get the matter off her conscience was to go down to the police station the following morning and tell them everything—

What was that?

Cassie bolted upright in bed, trying to identify the sound. A dog barked just outside her window, and then she heard a woman's voice. She relaxed at the

sound. She knew who it was. Mrs. Ambrose-Pritchard, the guest in Suite 3C, was taking her Maltese, Chablis, for a late evening stroll.

Across the room, Mr. Bogart got up from his bed and trotted to the window to peer out into the darkness. He turned to Cassie and began to whimper.

"The power of suggestion, huh?" Cassie fluffed her pillow. "Well, too bad, buddy. You'll just have to wait until morning."

The dog pawed frantically at the glass, then turned and raced into the living room where she could hear him scratch at the door.

"I'm not taking you out," she called.

He began to yelp, then howl, and after a moment, Cassie heard a series of soft thuds that sounded as if he might be throwing himself against the door.

"Oh, all right already," Cassie grumbled as she swung her legs over the side of the bed. Dressing quickly in jeans and a T-shirt, she pulled a baseball cap over her hair and clipped Mr. Bogart's leash to his collar. Then off they went.

They took the elevator down to the lobby, and Cassie kept her face averted as she nodded briefly to the night clerk behind the desk. Outside, she wanted to go right, but Mr. Bogart insisted on going left. Rolling her eyes, Cassie let him take the lead, but when they came to the alley, she balked.

"Uh-uh. Not no way, no how," she told the Chi-

huahua. "Don't you remember what happened the last time we went down that road? You got a boot up your little—"

Mr. Bogart jerked on the leash with such ferocity that Cassie was caught off guard. The leash slipped through her fingers, and the little dog took off like a shot.

"Why do you keep doing that?" she shouted behind him. This time, she wasn't going to follow him. She didn't care what Celeste said. That alley was teeming with perverts.

A moment later, Mr. Bogart came trotting out of the alley with a little white mop in tow. The rhinestone leash dragging behind the Maltese glittered in the light from the street, and Cassie stared at the dog in surprise. "Chablis? Is that you?"

Ignoring Cassie, the Maltese sat down and panted delicately in the heat as she watched Mr. Bogart spin in circles, chasing his tail and yapping in doggie-speak, "Look what I can do!"

"You're hot," Chablis's rapturous gaze seemed to imply.

"Sorry to interrupt this love fest," Cassie said dryly, "But where's your mommy, Chablis?"

Just then, Cassie heard something that sounded like a groan coming from the alley. Her pulse quickened as she peered into the shadows. "Who's there?"

The groan came again, louder this time, and then

a woman's shaky voice called, "Help! Please, someone help me…"

The two dogs turned and raced back into the alley with Cassie close on their heels. Mrs. Ambrose-Pritchard lay just beyond the overhang of Cassie's balcony. She'd propped herself against the wall of the hotel as she massaged her left ankle. When she saw Cassie, she let out a cry of relief. "Oh, thank God! I was afraid I might have to lie here until morning."

Cassie rushed over and knelt beside her. "What happened?"

Mrs. Ambrose-Pritchard was a tiny, wiry woman with a smooth cap of red hair, intrepid blue eyes and an imperious demeanor that could be, Cassie suspected, a bit terrifying at times. She was probably in her late fifties, but her face had been so carefully nipped and tucked that only the slightest tilt of her eyes gave away the work and her age.

"He came at me like a crazed animal!" she exclaimed, but Cassie couldn't tell if the woman's shrillness was due to fright or outrage. "I thought he was going to kill me!" She gazed around frantically. "Chablis! Where's my baby?"

"She's right here," Cassie assured her. "But who attacked you, Mrs. Ambrose…Pritchard…?" She trailed off awkwardly, uncertain how to address the woman. "Did you get a look at him?"

"No, not really." The tiny woman shuddered.

"And I'm thankful for that, or else I know I would have seen that face in my sleep tonight. I only caught a glimpse of him over there, just beneath your balcony. When I called out...he rushed toward me. Came at me so quickly I didn't know what to do. He could have had a knife or a gun..."

"You're safe now," Cassie murmured. "What did he do to you?" she tried to ask tactfully.

"He shoved me so hard I fell down, and then he fled that way—" Mrs. Ambrose-Pritchard pointed toward the rear of the hotel.

"How badly are you hurt?"

"It's my ankle. I don't think I can walk, and like a fool, I left my cell phone in my suite. Thank God you came along when you did or else he might have—" She broke off with a gasp, and her eyes widened as her gaze lifted to a point beyond Cassie's shoulder.

It was only then that Cassie saw the shadow looming on the wall above the injured woman.

Someone had come up behind them.

Chapter Three

The diminutive woman let out a scream that was so earsplitting Cassie froze for a moment. Her last coherent thought before she braced herself for the attack was that every small animal within a five-mile radius had probably keeled over at that sound. Including poor Mr. Bogart and little Chablis.

But, no. The two infatuated canines were still very much conscious and gazing up at the newcomer with nothing more than idle curiosity.

All this went through Cassie's mind in the blink of an eye as she whirled and prepared to defend herself. Then the man said in a rush, "Mrs. Ambrose-Pritchard! What on earth…"

"Lyle? Is that you skulking about over there? You scared me half to death!" the older woman scolded.

"I'm so sorry," he said contritely. "But…what happened? Why are you on the ground?"

"Why do you think? I've had a bad fall." In the space of a heartbeat, Mrs. Ambrose-Pritchard's tone

had gone from fearful to caustic, and the newcomer seemed to be the source of her irritation.

Cassie glanced at the woman in surprise. Then, her heart still racing, she transferred her gaze to the man hovering over them. He was youngish, some-where around thirty, with a slim build, brown hair styled in the latest shag, and even in the dark, Cassie could tell that his clothing—black on black—had a European flair.

She didn't know why, but when he returned her scrutiny, she found herself shrinking away from him.

"Miss Fortune? I'm sorry. I didn't recognize you at first."

Cassie frowned. "Do I know you?"

"I'm Lyle. Lyle Lester. The night manager? We haven't formally met, but I'm…a big admirer of yours."

That was a first. Celeste was still a relatively un-known actress, or at least, she had been until the scandal with Owen Fleming broke. Cassie hadn't considered the possibility that she might actually come face-to-face with some of her cousin's fans. She was at a loss as to how she should respond. "That's…nice."

Mrs. Ambrose-Pritchard said impatiently, "Lyle, if you could stop salivating for half a minute, perhaps you could give me a hand."

"Yes, of course, but…you say you fell? I do hope nothing is broken." His tone implied that a fractured

hip might not be out of the realm of possibility for someone of Mrs. Ambrose-Pritchard's advanced age. Evidently, the hostility went both ways, and Cassie couldn't help wondering about the pair's history.

"Actually, she was attacked," Cassie said.

He glanced up in alarm. "Attacked? By whom?"

"I didn't ask his name," the older woman snapped. "Nor did I get a good look at him. It all happened too quickly."

"Oh, dear, are you sure you're all right? Perhaps we should call an ambulance. After all, one can't be too careful…" *At your age.*

"No need for that." Mrs. Ambrose-Pritchard's tone was positively frigid by now. "I'm not the frail old lady you seem to think I am. If you would just help me up…"

But, in spite of her bravado, it soon became obvious that she needed a good deal more than a hand up. She couldn't put any weight on her ankle, nor was she able to balance herself using Lyle as a crutch. "Allow me," he said with a little half bow, then, despite his thin stature, swept the woman into his arms with no effort whatsoever. He was much stronger than he looked, and he walked with the kind of grace and agility that made Cassie think of a dancer.

She expected the older woman to protest, but instead Mrs. Ambrose-Pritchard peered over Lyle's shoulder into the shadows. "Where's my Chablis?" she demanded. "I can't leave her out here. She's

probably frightened half to death, poor baby. I doubt either one of us will get a wink of sleep tonight."

"I'll bring her along," Cassie said, reaching for the Maltese, who did not look in the least distressed by the evening's events. If anything, she appeared thoroughly besotted as she gazed at Mr. Bogart with doe-eyed intensity. When Cassie had finally corralled the dogs, the pair happily cavorted side by side back to the hotel.

The whole party took the elevator to the third floor, and after Mrs. Ambrose-Pritchard handed Cassie her key card, she unlocked the door and held it open while Lyle carried the injured woman inside and placed her gently on a green silk divan.

"Are you sure you won't go to the emergency room?" he asked anxiously.

Mrs. Ambrose-Pritchard gave him a scornful glance. "You can stop all that fussing. I don't intend to sue. I'm not the litigious sort."

Lyle assumed a wounded air. "A lawsuit was the furthest thing from my mind. My only concern is for you."

"How sweet." She made no attempt to hide the sarcasm in her tone. "You'll be happy to know, then, that I have a friend in town whose husband is an orthopedic surgeon. Rest assured if the ankle isn't better by morning, I'll give him a call. Now be a good boy and run along." She shooed him off with the back of her hand. "I don't need a thing more from you tonight."

"In that case," he said huffily, "I should get back to my desk."

"Wait a second. Both of you, just hold on a minute," Cassie said.

They examined her with surprise, as if they'd forgotten all about her presence.

"Don't you think we should call the police?" she asked.

"The police?" they repeated in unison.

Cassie frowned. "Yes, the police. You were attacked, Mrs. Ambrose. I mean, Mrs. Pritchard...Mrs. Ambrose-Pritchard—"

"Oh, for heaven's sake, just call me Evelyn."

Cassie nodded gratefully. "You said you were afraid your assailant was going to kill you."

"Did I say that?" The woman shifted on the sofa. "I was distraught and in a great deal of pain. I'm afraid I may have overreacted. But there's no need to involve the police."

"I think there is," Cassie insisted. "I don't know if either of you are aware of this or not, but a woman was murdered a few blocks from here tonight. And earlier, I saw a strange man lurking in the alley. He could have been your attacker...or even the killer."

"Oh, dear," Lyle murmured. He gave Cassie a sheepish grin. "I'm afraid you may have seen me." At her surprised look, he nodded. "I was in the alley earlier. As a matter of fact, I saw you standing on your balcony."

Was that why he looked familiar to her? Cassie wondered. They hadn't met until tonight, but perhaps she'd caught glimpses of him around the hotel. "Do you mind telling me why you were out there?"

"Not at all. There's really no mystery to it. Some of the kitchen staff saw someone going through the Dumpsters. I assumed it was Old Joe and decided to go out and have a look for myself."

"Old Joe?" Cassie asked doubtfully.

"He's harmless. He stays in a shelter on Montrose, but every now and then he drops by here to go through the trash. If I'm on duty, I give him a hot meal and a little cash, and he disappears, sometimes for weeks or months at a time. I wanted to head him off tonight before someone called the police. He can be a nuisance, but as I said, he's harmless and I'd hate to see him hauled off to jail. Poor old guy isn't in the best of health."

And she'd attacked him with her purse, Cassie thought guiltily. Although she didn't have the impression that Old Joe was exactly ancient or fragile. Judging by the way he'd sprinted down that alley, he still had a lot of life left in him.

"Well, that explains everything," Mrs. Ambrose-Pritchard said in satisfaction. "Undoubtedly, this Joe person is the man I encountered in the alley."

"But you said he attacked you," Cassie reminded her. "I'd hardly call that harmless."

"Perhaps he didn't mean to. I probably frightened the poor creature half to death, and when he tried to flee, he knocked me down."

It was a logical explanation, but Cassie's suspicions were aroused. She had *her* reasons for not wanting to involve the police, but what were Mrs. Ambrose-Pritchard's? Or Lyle's?

"Well, now that everything has been cleared up, I really do have to get back to work." He turned to Cassie. "I'll have another look in the alley just to make sure nothing is amiss, and I'll alert the staff to be on the lookout for any strangers lurking about the hotel. If anyone notices anything the least bit out of the ordinary, we'll notify the proper authorities immediately."

"Thank you."

After he left the room, Mrs. Ambrose-Pritchard fell back against the cushions and sighed. "That man is exhausting."

"I should go, too, and let you get some rest. You've had quite an ordeal tonight," Cassie said. "Is there anything I can get you before I leave?"

"I wouldn't mind a shot of vodka," the woman said candidly.

"Shall I call room service for you?"

"No, there's ice in the bucket and a bottle of Cristall in the fridge. I know Grey Goose is all the rage with you young folks, but I'm old-fashioned. I like my champagne French and my vodka Russian."

Cassie listened idly as she filled a glass with ice, poured in a generous amount of vodka, then carried the drink to the injured woman.

Mrs. Ambrose-Pritchard took a sip and sighed. "Oh, that hits the spot. The Russians do know their vodka. One can almost forgive them for that messy little affair in Cuba back in '62…"

Cassie didn't have the faintest idea what the woman was talking about. "Is there anything else I can get you?"

Mrs. Ambrose-Pritchard eyed her over the rim of her glass. "You don't remember me, do you?"

"Of course, I do. We met briefly in the lobby a few days ago."

"We met before that," the woman said slyly. "But I could tell you didn't remember."

Cassie's pulse quickened. First Lyle Lester and now Mrs. Ambrose-Pritchard. Evidently, her cousin wasn't quite as unknown as she'd let on to Cassie. And what was it Celeste had told her on the phone that day? *"Don't worry about running into friends or acquaintances at the Mirabelle. Most of the people I know could never afford to stay there."*

"I'm sorry," Cassie murmured, not really knowing what else to say.

Mrs. Ambrose-Pritchard shrugged off the apology. "Oh, don't be. I'm not surprised you don't remember. It was a brief encounter. We were on the same elevator a few months ago at the Beverly Hills

Hotel. The only reason I recall it so vividly is because your little dog there and Chablis got on so famously. We even joked about it being the beginning of a beautiful friendship. Does that ring a bell?"

The woman looked so hopeful that Cassie nodded. "Of course. I remember now. You had on the most gorgeous outfit that day. Chanel, wasn't it?" It was a stab in the dark, but since Mrs. Ambrose-Pritchard always dressed impeccably, Cassie thought it a safe guess.

"As a matter of fact, it was. How sweet of you to notice." Mrs. Ambrose-Pritchard took another sip of her vodka. When she glanced up, her eyes glinted with something that might have been mischief. Or malice. "It was only later, of course, that I realized…forgive me, I don't mean to be indelicate…but you were meeting Owen that day, weren't you?"

Cassie gasped. She couldn't help herself. "You know Owen Fleming?"

The woman smiled. "Small world, isn't it?" Then her expression sobered. "Owen and my late husband were business partners for a number of years until Thomas caught him, literally, with his hand in the till. Turned out, he'd embezzled millions from the company, and it took Thomas years to straighten out his finances, not to mention his good reputation. A word to the wise, my dear." She sat up and leaned toward Cassie. "Owen Fleming is a man completely without scruples. I don't know how Margo has put up

with him all these years, but I expect, in the end, she'll have her revenge."

"What do you mean?" Cassie asked almost fearfully.

"You see, Margo is originally from Chicago. Her mother's maiden name was Gambini. Does that mean anything to you?"

"Sounds Italian," Cassie murmured.

"Sicilian. The Gambinis control the most powerful crime syndicate in the Midwest. Margo may have moved away years ago, but she is still Family and the Gambinis always take care of their own. If I were you, dear, I'd watch my back. Not that it will do you any good. The Family employs experts for that sort of thing. *Wet work,* I believe they call it. You wouldn't even hear them coming…"

JUST WHAT THE HELL had Sissy gotten her involved in? Cassie wondered nervously as she let herself and Mr. Bogart into the suite. After she'd unclipped his leash, he ran over anxiously to check out the food and water situation before heading off to bed.

Cassie wished her own concerns were so basic. Okay, so the man hiding behind the Dumpster and the one below her balcony had been explained by Lyle Lester, but instead of resting easier, now she had to worry about a Mafia hit man coming after her. Her cousin had said nothing about ties to the Gambini crime family. As anxious as Cassie had been to put

distance between herself and the Cantrells, she was pretty sure that she would have remembered something like that.

So what was she supposed to do now? Call the whole thing off? Go crawling back to Manville with her tail tucked between her legs? Shove all her dreams back into the Payless shoe box where she'd kept them for the past ten years?

She couldn't do it. She'd waited too long to start her new life. Returning to her hometown just wasn't an option, Cassie decided. Besides, the threat of a Mafia hit man paled in comparison to facing Minnie Cantrell's wrath. The old woman was a witch in every sense of the word. She claimed to have not only the power to remove warts and divine water, but could also hex, conjure spirits and wreak all manner of havoc on those who crossed her or her kin.

Cassie had never personally witnessed any of the woman's powers, nor did she believe in them. But there were plenty in her hometown who did, and once Minnie Cantrell cursed you, you might as well pack it in. You became a pariah in the community, a social outcast to be shunned and scorned, and if there was anything worse than being stuck in the sticks, it was being stranded there without a single friend to your name.

Cassie had wanted to leave for years. For as long as she could remember, she'd dreamed of moving to Houston or New Orleans, settling into her own little

place and getting a job at an art gallery where she might someday exhibit her own work. But while her mother had still been alive, Cassie couldn't leave Manville.

Her mother was gone now, after losing a long battle with lung cancer and emphysema, and there was no one left from the Boudreaux clan—as ornery a bunch as the Cantrells—who Cassie felt any special affinity for. Celeste's call had come at a most opportune time. The art department at Manville High School had suffered major budgetary cuts, which meant that most of Cassie's classes had been dropped from the fall schedule. When the school district declined to renew her contract, she'd suddenly found herself unemployed, unattached and just itching for an adventure.

Be careful what you wish for, her mother had always warned.

"Good advice, Mama," Cassie murmured as she headed off for bed. She'd just slid under the covers when the phone on the nightstand rang. She hesitated to answer at first, then figuring it might be Lyle checking to make sure everything was okay, she picked up the receiver.

"Hello?" she said carefully.

"You are a hard woman to track down," a female voice accused.

Cassie didn't have a clue as to the woman's identity, but she tensed, anyway. "Who is this?"

"Who is this?" the woman asked incredulously. "It's Olivia. Olivia D'Arby? You know, your roommate? The girl you left holding the bag when you skipped out on the rent?"

Roommate? What roommate? Celeste had said nothing about a roommate.

The whole situation was getting more complicated by the minute. And it had sounded so simple at first. Spend a month in a luxury hotel pretending to be her cousin, and in return she would be treated to a new wardrobe, a little cash and ample opportunity to decide what she wanted to do with the rest of her life.

But now, in addition to everything else, a mysterious roommate was calling, and if Cassie said or did anything the least bit suspicious, the whole scheme could unravel. And she had a bad feeling that if that happened, she would be the one left holding the bag.

"Well? Aren't you even going to ask how I found you?" the woman demanded.

Cassie's hand gripped the phone. "How?"

"You left your itinerary on the computer. Not too smart for someone in hiding. What if the press or Margo Fleming had somehow gotten hold of it? But don't worry," she rushed to assure Cassie. "I deleted everything."

"Thanks."

Olivia paused. "What's wrong? You sound kind of strange."

Cassie cleared her throat, then lowered her voice. "I think I'm coming down with something."

"You're sick? Well, that's the least of your worries." Cassie couldn't detect even a drop of sympathy in the woman's voice. "That's why I'm calling. Some guy's been around asking a lot of questions about you. He talked to some of the neighbors, and he managed to corner me in the parking lot yesterday when I got back from my interview. Since I didn't get the part, I wasn't exactly in a friendly mood. He got an earful, but I don't think it was what he was after. Anyway, I thought you'd probably want to know what she's up to now."

"She?"

"Margo Fleming, of course. Who else would have sent that guy?" Olivia hesitated again. "Are you sure you're okay? You seem kind of out there. Maybe you're taking too much medication or something."

"I'm fine," Cassie rasped. "Thanks for the call."

"Wait a minute, damn it. You can't just blow me off like that. I went to all the trouble of tracking you down, the least you can do is give me the juicy details."

Juicy details? What was she talking about?

"Oh, I get it." Olivia's tone dropped conspiratorially. "He's there, isn't he?"

"Who?"

"Oh, for the love of...*Owen*. Remember him? Your rich, married lover? The man who gave you that huge diamond and promised to make you a star?"

Was that resentment Cassie heard in the woman's voice?

"Since I saw him first, the least you can do is be straight with me."

Definitely resentment, Cassie decided.

"Is he there with you or not?" Olivia persisted.

"I'm alone."

"I don't believe you. You leave town in the middle of the night, and a few days later, Owen disappears. You can't tell me that's a coincidence."

Cassie had no intention of telling her anything. All she wanted to do was get off the phone, *pronto,* before she said something to tip her hand. Honestly, what had Celeste been thinking when she left her itinerary on the computer? She must have known her roommate would find it.

Or…was that the point? Was this some sort of test? Maybe Olivia D'Arby was in on the ruse, and she was calling to make sure that Cassie didn't cave under pressure.

"I appreciate the call, but I'm not feeling well." Cassie lowered her voice to a hoarse whisper. "I really think I should get to bed."

"You do that," Olivia said coolly. "But if Margo Fleming shows up at your door, don't say I didn't warn you. I shudder to think what that woman is capable of."

Was that a note of glee she detected in the roommate's voice now? Cassie wondered.

WELL, SHE'D FLUNKED that little test, now hadn't she? Evelyn thought gleefully.

It was just as she'd suspected. The woman was a complete fraud.

The whole story about their chance encounter in an elevator at the Beverly Hills Hotel had been a spur-of-the-moment fabrication. There had been no Chanel outfit and certainly no quip about the beginning of a beautiful friendship between Chablis and that…that horrid little dog she called Mr. Bogart.

"As if my princess would ever show the slightest interest in such a creature," Evelyn crooned. Chablis's responding sigh was one of pure bliss. Undoubtedly she was dreaming about Zoë von Hendenburg's shih tzu or William Kendall's Lhasa apso. But a Chihuahua?

Evelyn shuddered. Over her dead body!

Still, the next few days promised to be…interesting. It was possible, of course, that the woman who had been in her suite earlier was, indeed, Celeste Fortune. Perhaps she'd pretended to remember the meeting in the elevator to spare Evelyn's feelings. After all, it was always awkward when one party remembered a brief encounter that the other did not.

And had that been the only incident, Evelyn might have been able to shrug it off in just that way.

But her suspicions had already been aroused before this evening, hence, the test.

Pleasantly buzzed from the vodka, Evelyn lay

back against the sofa and smiled as she recalled the night she'd first seen Celeste Fortune in person. A little birdie had told her that the actress had booked herself into the Mirabelle, and so Evelyn had arrived ahead of her. She'd been waiting in the lobby behind a potted palm to get her first look.

Celeste had arrived in a cab, completely alone, wearing a cap pulled low over her face much as she had been tonight. She'd thought it a clever disguise, no doubt, but Evelyn, who was something of a movie buff, especially when it came to Owen's productions, would have recognized her even without being tipped off. Even without that infamous diamond sparkling on the woman's hand.

Evelyn had followed her up to the third floor and observed her from a discreet distance as the bellman let her into her room. A few minutes later, a maid carrying a stack of fresh towels got off the elevator and knocked on Celeste's door.

Evelyn remembered the incident vividly because there had been something a little strange about the maid's appearance. For one thing, she'd worn a really bad wig.

And she'd seemed nervous. She kept glancing over her shoulder until Celeste had let her in.

Evelyn had watched in amazement as the woman came out a few minutes later and headed straight for the elevator. Again, Evelyn's attention was drawn to the wig. It looked slightly askew, as if she'd pulled

it on in a hurry, but the real giveaway was the Boucheron diamond glittering on the woman's finger. No maid owned a rock like that.

It was obvious to Evelyn that the two women had switched places, but why? And who was the imposter in Suite 3A pretending to be Celeste Fortune?

Where was the real Celeste? Off somewhere romantic and exotic with Owen?

It would be just like that bastard to plan such an elaborate scheme so that he could steal away for a few days with his mistress. And the real kick in the teeth? His devoted wife was probably picking up the tab for the whole affair.

Hands trembling in outrage, Evelyn carefully removed her own wig. Setting it aside, she smoothed back white tufts of hair as she reached for the phone.

Chapter Four

Cassie could barely contain her excitement. Metro was one of the trendiest, not to mention priciest, restaurants in the Montrose-Westheimer area, and from what she'd seen so far, worth every penny.

Easy to say, of course, considering her cousin was picking up the tab.

Dinner at Metro was one of the outings Celeste had arranged, and despite lying awake half the night worrying about the conversations she'd had with Mrs. Ambrose-Pritchard and Olivia D'Arby, Cassie had been looking forward all day to finally spending an evening away from the hotel.

The restaurant catered primarily to the arts and theater crowd, and as she gazed around, Cassie still had a hard time believing that she was actually there, seated on the terrace and blending into the bohemian atmosphere as if she truly belonged.

She sighed happily. This was the Houston she'd longed to discover since she'd arrived in town over

a week ago. The museums, the bistros and art galleries, the colorful parade of people along the streets. She wanted to be a part of it all.

Oh, my, she thought with a slight shock as she watched a chicly dressed transvestite sashay by in an exquisite pair of Manolo Blahniks. *You would not see that in Manville.*

You wouldn't see a lot of things in Cassie's hometown, which was why she'd been hankering to get out ever since she'd graduated from high school. Her mother had gotten sick, though, during Cassie's senior year, and she'd stayed home to take care of her and to watch from afar as her cousin had gone off to first Houston, and then Hollywood, to seek fame and fortune.

Cassie hadn't been jealous. Truly, she hadn't. She was happy for Sissy's success. And she didn't begrudge the time she'd spent caring for her mother. The two of them had been very close, and Cassie still mourned her loss.

But at the same time, she couldn't help luxuriating in her newfound liberty. Her mother's death had freed her in more ways than one. It had allowed her to take a long, hard look at her life and to decide once and for all which parts were worth keeping and which ones needed to be tossed away.

Her schoolteacher's wardrobe had been the first to go.

Danny Cantrell had been the second.

Even now, Cassie felt a prickle of guilt for the way she'd broken things off with him. She should have worked up her courage long before they'd arrived at the church, but it wasn't like Danny had taken her decision all that hard. Mostly, he'd just been hungover from the night before.

Only after his family had goaded him had he and his friends started harassing Cassie. All of a sudden, she'd had a rash of flat tires and threatening phone calls, and after Earl Cantrell had almost run her down one morning, she knew it was time for a change.

So here she was.

She placed her order with a very cute waiter and contentedly sipped her Grey Goose vodka—thank you, Mrs. Ambrose-Pritchard—cocktail as she watched the street. A few minutes later, her attention was distracted by a man seated a few tables over from her. When she glanced in his direction, she caught him staring at her.

Quickly, she averted her gaze, wondering if he was coming on to her.

Maybe he simply found her attractive, she decided. After all, that wasn't such a stretch, was it? She might not be in her cousin's league, but she wasn't exactly a carnival sideshow, either.

And tonight she looked especially stylish, if she did say so herself, in her new Diesel jeans and Juicy Couture T-shirt—also compliments of Celeste. Of course, those jeans were undoubtedly a size or two— or three—larger than her cousin normally wore, but

Cassie wouldn't dwell on that evil. Instead, she glanced down at her feet, admiring the way her pink-polished toenails peeked out of her new Jimmy Choo slides.

A girl could get used to this life, she thought with an inward sigh.

And then in the next instant, as she stole another glance at the stranger, she wondered, *Does he think I'm her?* Not Celeste Fortune, necessarily, but a woman who could afford five-hundred-dollar shoes and Stella McCartney sunglasses and who knew which vodka to order and which sushi bar to frequent?

Or could he see right through her? Did he know she was a fake?

Cassie couldn't tell from his expression since he also wore sunglasses, but she knew he was looking at her. He was the kind of man who had always intimidated her a little because he so obviously came from a world she coveted. His hair was very short and very bleached, his dark glasses, ultracool and high tech. He had the look of an artist or a musician or even an actor, someone for whom the bohemian lifestyle was as natural as breathing. And his attitude was that of a man who didn't give a damn what the rest of the world thought of him.

Cassie was instantly smitten.

And wary. A man like that would undoubtedly be interested in Celeste Fortune, but plain old Cassie Boudreaux? Only when hell froze over.

Still watching her, he slowly removed his sunglasses, and when Cassie saw his blue eyes, a thrill raced up her backbone. She found herself reaching up to take off her own glasses.

And then their gazes met.

Clung.

It was like something from a movie, Cassie thought with another shiver. It was fate. Providence. Very good karma.

Hardly aware of what she was doing, she scooped an ice chip from her drink, ran it over her lips and slid it into her mouth.

His gaze on her deepened. And then very deliberately, he ringed the edge of his glass with his fingertip. When his finger dipped inside, a shudder went through Cassie's whole body.

Oh, my God, she thought in alarm. What was she doing?

HOLY—

Jack cut himself off and drew a deep breath. Were they doing what he thought they were doing?

So much for an inconspicuous surveillance, but hell, who cared? Celeste Fortune was *hot.*

And way out of your league, Jackie, he could hear Cher warn him.

Okay, okay, but she was *hot.* Her hair. Those eyes. Those…lips.

He groaned inwardly when she slid the ice cube

into her mouth yet again. If they kept this up, he wouldn't be walking out of this place with his dignity intact, that was for damn sure. If they kept this up—

A movement on the roof of the building across the street momentarily caught his attention and he glanced up with a frown. Something flashed in the deepening shadows, like light bouncing off glass. Or a rifle scope...

No sooner had the thought formed in his head than a shot rang out, and all hell broke loose on the terrace. A waitress dropped a tray of drinks and someone screamed.

Jack saw the terror in Celeste Fortune's eyes a split second before he dove.

CASSIE WAS MOMENTARILY frozen by shock and fear, and then it was she who screamed as the stranger hurled himself toward her. He slid across her table, tipping her chair backward, and they both went crashing to the floor.

She was frozen again, this time without breath. The stranger lay sprawled on top of her, his lips only inches from hers, his blue gaze peering into hers.

"Are you okay?" he asked anxiously.

Cassie still couldn't speak. All she could do was lie there gasping for air.

"You're not hurt, are you? Oh, God, you're not—"

"Can't…breathe…" she managed.

He rolled off her. "Stay down," he warned, and then he got to his feet, vaulted over the wrought-iron fence surrounding the patio, and sprinted into the street. A horn sounded, tires squealed, but he didn't seem to notice. In a matter of seconds, he'd disappeared into the traffic.

Cassie glanced around. She was the only one on the floor. In fact, a number of people had hurried over and stood staring down at her.

"It's okay," someone said. "It was just a car backfiring."

Nervous laughter erupted on the terrace.

Now that Cassie's initial fear had dissipated, mortification set in. "I thought it was a gunshot," she muttered as she struggled to her feet.

"So did I," the waitress who'd dropped the glasses said sheepishly. She reached to give Cassie a hand up.

"It was that old blue truck that just went by," someone commented. "I thought it was part of the Art Car parade at first, but then I realized it hadn't been painted to look that way. The metal was just all rusted. And it had Louisiana plates."

Cassie glanced up sharply. Danny's uncle drove an old rusty blue pickup, and he and his nephew were as thick as thieves. What if they'd come to Houston looking for Cassie?

But that was impossible. She hadn't told anyone

where she was going. That was part of her and Celeste's agreement. In order for the plan to work, no one could know where she was, so she'd packed up and left town in the middle of the night.

The rusty, blue truck had to be a coincidence. No way Danny and Earl could have found her so quickly and, besides, there wasn't a Cantrell alive who'd be caught dead in Montrose.

"Where'd your friend run off to?" the first waitress asked Cassie.

She tore her attention from the street. "He's…not my friend. I never saw him before."

"Maybe he was just embarrassed by the way he overreacted."

I think we both overreacted, Cassie thought, remembering the way his finger had slowly traced the edge of his glass. She felt that odd little shudder go through her again.

The waitress cocked her head as she studied Cassie. "Say, do I know you? You seem familiar." She snapped her fingers. "I know. You look like that actress. The one who was in—"

Cassie was spared from having to answer by the maître d' who pushed his way through the crowd. "Miss, are you okay?"

"Yes, I'm fine. Nothing hurt but my pride," Cassie tried to quip as she brushed off her two-hundred-dollar jeans.

"We'll get this mess cleaned up and have a new

table ready for you in a matter of moments. In the meantime, if you would care to wait at the bar…"

"Oh, I don't think I could eat a bite after all that excitement," Cassie said with a weak smile. "I'm still a little shaky. If I could just have my check?"

He waved her off. "It's on the house, of course. Please accept our sincerest apologies for the inconvenience."

As he escorted her from the terrace, Cassie heard the waitress say behind her, "She looks just like her! You know the one I mean. She was in that movie…damn, I can't think of her name…"

The maître d' walked Cassie through the restaurant and even accompanied her out to the street after taking the time to personally call her a cab.

"You don't have to wait with me," she assured him. "I'm perfectly fine." She felt a bit of what Mrs. Ambrose-Pritchard had experienced the night before with Lyle Lester. She wasn't sure if the man's solicitousness was truly out of concern for her safety or fear of an impending lawsuit.

Apparently convinced that he'd done everything he could to ward off such a threat, he wished her a good night and went back into the restaurant.

The cab showed up a few minutes later, and as Cassie climbed into the back, she glanced at the building across the street. For some reason, her gaze was drawn upward, and she saw someone standing on the roof looking down at her. In the split second

before he disappeared, she could have sworn he was the stranger from the restaurant.

But…what was he doing up there?

JACK WATCHED Celeste's cab drive off, then he turned his attention back to the roof. He hadn't found anything yet, but he knew what he'd seen. Light reflecting off glass. Someone had been up there. He was still convinced of that even though he'd realized by the time he was halfway across the street earlier that the sound he'd heard was a backfire and not a gunshot.

Besides, a professional hit man would have used a silencer.

Professional hit man? Whoa, hold the phone. Jumping to a few wild conclusions there, aren't you, buddy?

Who would want Celeste Fortune dead?

The cop in him silently began to list suspects. Owen Fleming's wife. An old boyfriend. A jealous roommate.

And that was just off the top of his head. He knew from experience the potential for animosity was endless when it came to women like Celeste Fortune.

But if someone had really been watching her earlier, the culprit was probably just some sleazy tabloid reporter who'd followed her to Houston, hoping to catch Owen Fleming in a compromising position with his hot, young mistress. What Jack had seen on the roof could have been light reflecting off a camera lens.

His theory made a lot of sense, and he might have been able to buy it if not for that nagging sensation in his gut telling him Celeste Fortune was in danger.

A similar sensation had warned him that Casanova was still on the loose, and look where that premonition had gotten him.

THE FRONT DESK was deserted when Cassie walked into the lobby a few minutes later. She wondered if Lyle Lester had come on duty yet, and if he might be lurking about somewhere. For some reason, the notion of him skulking about in the halls and stairwells made her shiver, and she hurried across the lobby into a waiting elevator.

The car began to ascend, then jerked to a stop when the power went out. Cassie was plunged into pitch black for a moment before a dim emergency light came on. Trying to remain calm, she pressed the red button on the panel, but nothing happened. She couldn't find a phone, either, so what was she supposed to do?

Panic! a little voice screamed in her head, but Cassie ignored it. No need for that. The power had simply gone off, and she was trapped somewhere between the first and second floor. It wasn't like she was in danger of plunging hundreds of feet to her death. If worse came to worst, she could try to reach that little door in the ceiling, climb out, and—

A soft thud sounded from somewhere above her,

and then the elevator shimmied as if...some-one...had...jumped...on top...

Slowly, Cassie lifted her gaze.

"Hello?" she called as her heart flailed against her chest. "Is someone up there?"

No answer. Everything was silent except for the sound of her own breathing.

She whirled back to the control panel and jammed the red emergency button with her thumb.

Stay calm, she warned herself.

To hell with that. Frantically, she began to push random buttons.

A split second later, the power came back on and with a slight shudder, the elevator continued its ascent to the third floor.

As Cassie got out, she turned and glanced at the panel in the ceiling. Had someone been up there? Was he still there?

With a little shriek, she jumped back as the elevator doors slid closed.

Letting herself into her suite, Cassie tried to convince herself that the whole thing had been her imagination, triggered by the incident at the restaurant. But when the phone rang, she jumped violently, and then scolding herself, rushed to answer it. She hoped it was Celeste. She had a few choice questions for her cousin, like why in the hell hadn't she mentioned the fact that a hit man might be on her tail?

"Did I scare you?" said an electronically altered voice in her ear.

The blood in Cassie's veins turned to ice as her hand squeezed the phone. "Who is this?"

"Open the door and find out."

The line went dead then, and as Cassie slowly turned toward the door, someone knocked.

Chapter Five

Cassie's gaze remained riveted on the door. There was no way she would answer it. No way in hell she would go anywhere near it—

The dead bolt! Had she locked it when she came in? She couldn't remember. The phone had started to ring. She'd been distracted—

She flew across the room and twisted the lock, but it was already engaged, thank goodness.

Was he still out there? Cassie wondered frantically.

Pressing her ear to the door, she heard nothing. Then, her heart still pounding, she glanced through the peephole. She couldn't see anything, either. Her tormentor might have cut and run or…he might be standing to the side of the door, out of sight, hoping to lure her into the hall.

Cassie glanced over her shoulder at the phone, wondering if she should call the front desk or even the police. But what would she tell them? That some-

one had played a prank on her? Because that's all it was, wasn't it? She couldn't actually be in danger, could she?

What if she was? What if Mrs. Ambrose-Pritchard was right, and Margo Fleming had called on her family to exact a little payback?

But…wouldn't a Mafia hit man be a little more subtle?

Come to think of it, though, subtlety had never been the Cantrells' strong suit.

When Cassie put her eye back to the peephole, someone stared back at her.

She gasped and jumped away from the door. Whoever was out there knocked again, more boldly this time, as if he didn't care who might hear him.

Cassie's hand flew to her chest. Her heart was racing so fast she could hardly catch her breath. "Who's there?" she called.

A male voice said anxiously, "Miss Fortune? It's Lyle…Lester. The night clerk said she saw you get on the elevator right before the power went off. I just wanted to make sure you're okay."

Then why hadn't he simply called her suite? Cassie wondered.

And how had the night clerk witnessed her getting onto the elevator? The girl hadn't even been at the desk when Cassie had come in.

"Miss Fortune?"

Cassie bit her lip. Then drawing a deep breath, she said, "I'm fine. No harm done."

"I'm so relieved to hear it. I've brought you up a flashlight and some candles. I heard on the news earlier that these outages are happening all over town. Something about an overloaded power grid caused by the heat wave. Hopefully, it'll just be temporary, but I thought it best to be prepared just in case."

Cassie stepped back up to the peephole. She couldn't tell what Lyle held in his hand, but she sure as hell wasn't about to open the door to find out.

"I'm…indisposed at the moment," she called. "Can you just leave the stuff outside the door?"

A slight hesitation, then, "Of course. If you need anything else, please let us know."

"I will."

Cassie's eye was still pressed to the peephole, and as Lyle Lester walked away, she saw him pause once and glance over his shoulder before he disappeared from her view.

JACK PULLED a dark cap over his head and rubber boots onto his feet, then headed for the Dumpsters behind the Mirabelle. He'd bribed a maid to mark an X in red tape on the trash bags that came from Celeste's suite, so he had high hopes that his job would go more smoothly tonight.

He had to be careful, though. Now that Celeste

had gotten a good look at him, he couldn't chance running into her again. He was damn lucky she hadn't recognized him from the night before, but he supposed he had Cher to thank for that.

At any rate, it had been stupid and amateurish to follow her into that restaurant. The pricey menu and trendy decor were about as far out of his league as she was, and besides, it was never a good idea to get that close to a mark. It really wasn't a good idea to get too close…to her.

But Jack had conducted enough surveillance operations to recognize the symptoms. It was the Stockholm Syndrome in reverse. Spending so much time observing from afar, the watcher began to identify with the subject to the point of infatuation. Sometimes the temptation to see her up close and personal became irresistible. Sometimes he would even fantasize about getting to know her, about protecting her…

That had to be it. How else to explain his feelings for Celeste Fortune? Love at first sight?

There was a time when Jack would have been the first to scoff at such a notion, but not after the Casanova case. Not after he'd seen with his own two eyes how five sophisticated and successful women had been swept off their feet by a suave and sadistic killer.

Love at first sight? Loneliness? The thrill of a stranger's seduction? Who knew what had moti-

vated those women to invite a killer into their homes after they'd taken the time to carefully set the stage for romance?

The criminal psychologist called in to consult on the case had been convinced that Casanova stalked his victims for weeks, possibly months before he approached them. According to Dr. West, the killer had gotten to know his targets inside and out—their hopes and dreams, their deepest fears and darkest fantasies. And then he used those intimacies to seduce them.

He'd probably even gone through their trash, Jack thought in disgust as he pulled out a plastic bag marked with a red X. He dropped the bag on the ground and grimaced.

What was he doing?

Just what the hell was he doing?

He was a cop, for God's sake. The fact that he'd been kicked off the force didn't change who he was. *What* he was. A man who'd sworn not only to uphold the law, but to serve and protect.

This wasn't serving anybody but himself and some rich geek who couldn't get a woman on his own merits. So he'd stooped to this level and so had Jack. He'd allowed his financial and professional setbacks to cloud his judgment. He'd used his desperation to catch a killer as an excuse to trade in his ethics.

And in the process, he'd become someone he didn't much like or respect.

Well, it stopped now, he decided as he picked up the trash bag from Celeste's room and slung it back into the Dumpster. As he turned away in self-loathing, he heard something rattle in the alley.

He froze. For the longest moment, he listened to the darkness, but when he heard nothing else, he figured it must have been his imagination or a rat scurrying through the trash.

Then he heard a bumping sound, and leaving the Dumpsters, he flattened himself against the wall of the hotel and peered down the alley. He saw nothing at first, but then farther down, near the street, something moved underneath a third-floor balcony.

Hugging the wall, Jack slipped silently into the alley. As he drew closer, he recognized the sound he'd heard earlier. A grappling hook had been thrown over the balcony railing of Celeste's suite, and a slender figure clad in black was now shimmying up the rope.

Drawing his weapon, Jack sprinted from the shadows. "Police! Halt!"

The suspect spun, saw him, then doubling his efforts, scurried the rest of the way up before Jack could reach him. Climbing over the railing, the intruder pulled the rope up behind him, then turned and tried the French doors.

Jack took aim as he raced toward the balcony. "Freeze!"

The suspect—his face covered by a ski mask—

glanced back at Jack, then slung the grappling hook all the way to the roof. It caught on a drainpipe, and as nimble as an acrobat, he scampered up.

A dozen scenarios flashed through Jack's head, none of them good. If he fired his weapon, there would be hell to pay. Impersonating a police office carried a stiff sentence, and considering the animosity he'd left behind at police headquarters and city hall, he couldn't imagine anyone coming down on his side.

Still, it wasn't hard to figure that a guy wearing a ski mask and wielding a grappling hook in the middle of the night was up to no good. It was obvious he'd meant to get in Celeste's suite, but for what purpose, Jack could only imagine.

The intruder had almost made it to the roof by this time. Grasping the edge, he hitched himself over, then scrambled to his feet. Pausing for a moment, he gazed over the edge.

Jack had him in his sights. He could have easily taken him out, but he didn't. Instead he slowly lowered his weapon.

There was something familiar about him…her…

Something that sent a shiver up Jack's spine as their gazes met in the darkness.

Then, with a mocking salute, the intruder turned and disappeared over the slope of the roof.

JACK RANG THE BELL, then banged loudly on Max Tripp's door until a light came on in the town house.

A few minutes later, his ex-partner drew back the door.

Max looked shocked when he saw the bandage wrapped around Jack's hand. "What happened to you?"

Jack brushed past him. "We need to talk."

"So you said on the phone." Max closed the door and turned. He looked as if he'd dressed in a hurry and in the dark. He wore a pair of sweatpants and an old HPD T-shirt that might have served double duty as a cleaning rag. His disheveled appearance was a far cry from the slick image he presented at his posh offices on South Post Oak, and for a moment, Jack was relieved to see the man he'd known years ago. Maybe this Max would be willing to listen to reason.

But his next words didn't instill much hope. "This had better be good." Reluctantly, he gestured toward the living room.

"It is," Jack said grimly as they both took seats. "She's in danger, Max."

"Who's in danger?"

"Celeste Fortune." Jack ran a hand through his hair. "I'm not the only one tailing her. I've been getting a strange vibe ever since I started the surveillance, but tonight I actually saw someone try to break into her suite. You know what this means, don't you?"

Max's frowned deepened. "What?"

Restless, Jack got up and began to pace. "We have to warn her."

"Now hold on a minute." Max's gaze tracked him to and fro. "Let's not make any hasty decisions here. Just calm down and tell me exactly what you saw."

"It started when I followed her to a restaurant on Montrose tonight." Quickly, Jack explained about the flash of light on the building across the street.

Max shrugged after he'd heard him out. "So? You said yourself you didn't find anything. More than likely what you saw was light reflecting off a window in the building."

"No, I'm positive it came from the roof. And then when I went back to the hotel a little while later, I saw someone climb up to her balcony. He tried to get into her room, but the door was locked. If I hadn't been there to scare him off, he probably would have broken the glass. God only knows what he meant to do once inside." The images swirling around in Jack's head made him feel sick. If he hadn't been there— "The point is, she's obviously in danger and we have to warn her."

"I'm afraid we can't do that."

Jack stopped pacing and glared down at Max. "What do you mean we can't do that? If anything happens to her, it'll be on our conscience."

Max shrugged again. "Then that's a chance we'll have to take. If we go to her now, it'll blow the whole operation. We can't do it. Our loyalty is to the client."

"Like hell it is," Jack said angrily. "We're cops, for God's sake."

"*Were* cops. That's the operative word," Max re-

minded him. His expression hardened. "Look, I know you always took that 'to serve and protect' stuff to heart, but you're not on the force anymore. You work for me now, and I thought we had an understanding."

Jack couldn't believe what he was hearing. "A woman's life is at stake. That supercedes any agreement we had."

Max calmly folded his arms across his chest. "You don't know that her life is in danger. You're jumping to conclusions. The guy you saw tonight was probably a run-of-the-mill burglar or a two-bit jewel thief after that huge rock Fleming bought her. Now that you've scared him off, I doubt he'll be back."

Jack wasn't so sure about that. The guy knew what he was doing. By the time Jack had found a way up to the roof, the suspect had disappeared without a trace. He couldn't have escaped so easily unless he knew his way around that hotel backward and forward.

Jack hadn't so much as caught a glimpse of him. All he'd gotten for his trouble was a bad scrape on a rusty nail. And just his luck, he didn't remember when he'd had his last tetanus shot.

"If you're not going to do anything about this, then I'll take care of it myself," he said. "I've still got a few favors I can call in downtown."

Max gave him a shrewd appraisal. "And just what

are you going to tell them? That the woman you've been stalking is being stalked by someone else? The way I hear it, you've already been making a nuisance of yourself downtown trying to get information about that homicide in Montrose. Next thing you know, you'll be trying to convince them that Celeste Fortune is being stalked by Casanova."

Anger shot through Jack at the man's cold assessment. Something had happened to Max since he'd left the police department. Something that Jack didn't want to see when he looked at himself in the mirror every morning. "I'll tell them whatever I have to," he warned.

"Meaning?"

"I'll tell them I work for you."

Max stood. "You seemed to have forgotten that little thing called *a confidentiality agreement* that you signed the other day. You go shooting off your mouth about our business arrangement, and I'll deny ever having had this conversation with you. I'll say I threw a few odd jobs your way because I felt sorry for you. What you did with Celeste Fortune you did on your own. I've never even heard of her. Who do you think they're going to believe, Jack? Unlike you, I still have friends in high places."

Jack clenched his fists. "What the hell are you doing, Max? We were partners once."

"And we could be again, but you've got to forget about being a cop. That part of your life is over. I'm giving you a chance to make something of yourself,

but the first thing you have to learn about our business is that protecting our client's interests comes first."

Jack glanced at his ex-partner in disgust. "Sounds to me like covering your ass comes first."

Max walked over to the window and stared out for a moment, then turned. "Let me ask you something. Do you really think you were kicked off the force for ruffling too many feathers at city hall? Hell, you'd been doing that for years. But the brass put up with it because you were a good cop. They didn't want to lose you. So what changed?"

"You seem to have all the answers," Jack said coldly. "You tell me."

"They got rid of you because you scared them. You became so obsessed with the Casanova case that even guys who'd known you for years began to worry about your stability. An unbalanced cop is a dangerous entity, as we both know. You go down there now with a cockamamy story about some actress being stalked, what do you think they're going to do? Who do you think they're going to put under surveillance? It won't be Celeste Fortune."

"We'll see about that." Jack whirled and strode toward the door.

Behind him, Max said, "Did it ever occur to you that the best way to protect her is to keep doing what you're doing?" When Jack turned, Max continued grimly, "You've got a job to do, Jack. If someone

wants to harm Celeste Fortune, it's in our client's best interest to find out who that person is."

FROM HIS POSITION across the street, Jack could see the southeast corner of the hotel, including Celeste's balcony. The lights were off inside her suite so he assumed the earlier incident hadn't awakened her.

He hated to think of her up there sleeping peacefully in her bed with no inkling of the danger that could be lurking nearby.

And Jack couldn't tell her.

Max was right about that. *I know someone is stalking you because I've been stalking you myself.* Yeah, that'd go over big—with her and the police. He couldn't tell Celeste she was in danger any more than he could alert the cops because he'd be the one put under a microscope. So what the hell was he supposed to do?

After he left Max's place, Jack had toyed briefly with the idea of placing an anonymous call to the police, but he knew only too well how much good that would do. At the most, they'd send a patrol car to check out the alley and when they found nothing, the whole thing would be forgotten.

So it was up to Jack to protect her. Max was right about that, too. Jack had to keep doing what he was doing in order to watch out for her, but would that be enough? He couldn't spend twenty-four hours a day on surveillance. He couldn't shadow her every move.

Or…could he?

An idea came to him suddenly, and yanking his wallet from his pocket, he pulled out the check Max had given him a few days ago. An advance, he'd said, to get some nice clothes and a decent haircut.

Well, he had the haircut. And he knew that Cher, queen of resale shopping, could help him out with his wardrobe. Now all he had to do was book himself into the Mirabelle and strike up a friendship with Celeste. With any luck, he'd be able to catch her stalker in the act before his money ran out.

Settling in for the night, Jack slid down in the car seat, folded his arms, and began to plan a "coincidental" meeting with the gorgeous actress.

Chapter Six

Cassie lay atop the padded sundeck of a thirty-five-foot cabin cruiser and hoped this second outing Celeste had arranged for her would go more smoothly than the first.

So far everything had gone according to schedule. The rental car had arrived at the hotel that morning promptly at nine o'clock, and less than an hour later, Cassie had crossed the causeway on I-45 into Galveston.

She'd spent another half hour looking for Ethan Gold's house on Jamaica Beach, but she hadn't minded the search. From her very first glimpse of the Gulf, the tension had steadily melted away.

Now Cassie felt positively decadent, lying topless in the sun on her own boat. Well, okay, her own *borrowed* boat. The distinction didn't bother her one bit because she had two whole days to loll about in the sun and surf and pretend that this life really did belong to her.

Soon enough she'd have to come back to earth and start the old job search, but for now, this had to be one of her cousin's better ideas, she decided lazily.

According to Celeste, Ethan Gold, her old drama professor at the University of Houston, had insisted that she have the use of his beach house while she was in town. "There's a boat and everything," Celeste had told her. "I know how much you love to be out on the water."

Cassie had forgotten just how much she did love the fresh air and open sea. When she and Celeste were kids, their fathers had owned a fishing boat together, and on weekends and summers, the cousins had practically lived on the Gulf. They'd become expert swimmers early on—their fathers had seen to that—and had even learned to handle a boat by the ripe old age of eleven.

They'd become so proficient, in fact, that by the time they hit adolescence, they were taking the boat out alone, sometimes with permission and sometimes without.

The two had been as close as sisters back then, and those days were some of the happiest and most carefree of Cassie's life.

Then everything had changed. Celeste's family moved away, and Cassie's parents divorced. Her father relocated to Florida, and Cassie seldom heard from him. A few years later, her mother was diagnosed with emphysema and later, lung cancer. For al-

most a decade, it had been one trauma after another, and somewhere along the way, the carefree, adventurous Cassie had gotten lost in the harsh realities of life.

In her most vulnerable moments, she sometimes wondered how differently things might have turned out if her parents had stayed together. Would her mother still have gotten sick? Would Cassie, free of responsibilities, have had the nerve to pursue her dreams the way her cousin had?

She liked to think so, but she'd learned a long time ago that there was no profit in looking back. Besides, she had the rest of her life to work on those dreams, to try and recapture that old carefree Cassie, and now she had nothing to hold her back. No job. No fiancé. No responsibilities except to herself.

That was why she'd been so eager to accept Celeste's proposal. It wasn't just the money or the new clothes or the luxurious accommodations that had attracted her to the scheme. It was the scheme itself. The promise of adventure for which Cassie had been yearning a long, long time.

And so here she was. Footloose and fancy-free.

Well, almost.

There was the little matter of that threatening voice on the phone the other night.

"Did I scare you?"

Yes, as a matter of fact.

Every time Cassie thought about that anonymous

call, shivers stole up and down her spine. The person on the other end hadn't actually threatened her, but if the call had been nothing more than a prank, why had the caller gone to the trouble of electronically disguising his voice?

And afterward, Lyle Lester had shown up at Cassie's door.

True enough, he'd left a flashlight and candles outside her room, but his arrival had been extremely fortuitous. Could he have called her from the hallway on a cell phone? Cassie wondered. She'd received a couple of hang up calls since then, too. Was Lyle responsible for those as well?

He'd said the other night that he was an admirer, but just how big a fan was he? Had his appreciation crossed the line into psychotic obsession?

And speaking of psychotic…

Cassie frowned as an image of the stranger she'd seen at Metro materialized in her head. The more she thought about him—and she'd thought about him a lot—the more bizarre his behavior seemed. Everyone on the patio had reacted as though they'd heard a gunshot when the truck backfired. But rather than taking cover, the stranger had lunged straight for Cassie. Why? Why had he been so willing to put himself between her and a bullet? And, even more disturbing, why had he assumed she was the target?

In retrospect, Cassie had to admit that her own behavior that night had been a little on the bizarre side

as well. Coming on to a complete stranger was so totally unlike her.

But…was it really?

How did she know what she might be capable of?
It had been a long time since she'd had the opportunity to explore the real Cassie. For the past ten years,
she'd been a caregiver, a fiancée, and a schoolteacher, but none of those things had satisfied her
deepest yearnings, her darkest fantasies.

Somehow, the blue-eyed stranger had tapped into
her hidden desires, and for a fleeting moment, he'd
unleashed something wild inside of her. Something
at once familiar and strange.

He could give her adventure. She knew that instinctively.

He wasn't like any man she'd ever known. Certainly not like Danny. Her ex-fiancé could be an en-
thusiastic and ardent lover when the mood struck
him, but hardly an imaginative one.

Oh, he knew how to turn a woman on. He could
do that just by walking into a room. His bronzed, perfectly proportioned body had reduced stronger
women than Cassie to quivering masses of hor-
mones. But how quickly the charm faded once he
opened his mouth.

The stranger at Metro…he was hardly in Danny's
league looks-wise. He wasn't as tall or nearly as
good-looking, and his body had appeared leaner and
more sinewy rather than muscle-bound. But there

had been something about him…something sensuous and mysterious…

He had an air of having seen and done things that Cassie could only imagine. But she wanted to do more than imagine. She wanted to experience those things for herself.

After all, there had to be more to life than the missionary position, didn't there?

Resting her chin on her arms, she gazed around. It was a hot, still day. The water was unusually calm, which was why she'd decided to drop anchor and relax for a bit in the sun.

"You'll pay for that when you're forty," she could hear her mother scold her. Her mother hadn't so much as set foot outside without slathering on sunscreen, and even at the beach, she'd always worn a hat and long sleeves. But with all her precautions, Felicity Boudreaux had still died young, without ever having seen much of the world. Cassie didn't want that to be her fate.

She sighed, feeling melancholy, as she always did when she thought of her mother.

Glancing at her watch, she was surprised to find how long she'd already been out. She would need to head in soon, but for now it felt so good to be on the water after being cooped up in that hotel for over a week. Poor Mr. Bogart. She'd left him all alone at the beach house. To make up for it, she would take him for a nice, long walk on the beach

after dinner. Maybe then he'd stop pining for Chablis.

Cassie had tried to break it to him gently that the immaculately groomed Maltese was about as far out of his league as the guy at Metro was hers. But Mr. Bogart wouldn't listen. Evidently, Hollywood had gone to his little doggie head. Cassie could understand that. The good life suited her just fine, too.

As she watched the activity on the water, she noticed that another boat had anchored several hundred yards to the starboard side while she'd been daydreaming. Far enough away not to intrude on her privacy, but near enough that she felt a vague sense of unease. When she lifted her hand to shield her eyes, she saw someone fishing off the deck.

She reached behind her back to refasten her swimsuit straps, but as she lifted herself from the deck, an unexpected gust of wind caught the top and swept it away. It drifted on an air current for one brief moment before taking a header into the water.

Cassie stared at the bobbing fabric in dismay. Luckily, the extra padding kept it afloat.

"HO...LY..." Jack's muttering segued into a low whistle. He'd picked up his binoculars at precisely the right moment to catch a glimpse of a topless Celeste Fortune before she jumped into the water.

Stunned by the flash of skin, he quickly lowered the binoculars, warning himself that he was fast be-

coming little better than a Peeping Tom. But, pervert or not, he was also a red-blooded male with a half-naked woman in view. How the hell was he supposed to react to that? Ignore her? Look the other way?

He did what came naturally.

Adjusting his cap to keep the sun out of his eyes, he lifted the binoculars again and watched her strike out toward something blue that floated in the water several yards from her boat. Since he'd caught a glimpse of the same color before she hit the water, he assumed that it was her swimsuit top now drifting away on a current.

Man, could that girl swim.

For anyone else, that top would have been halfway to Mexico by now, but Celeste reached it easily. As she turned back to the boat, a wave caught and lifted her, and Jack was given another fortuitous peek before she struggled into her top.

Not bad.

Smaller than he would have thought from her pictures, but not bad at all. In fact, he'd say the view was pretty damn spectacular.

He would wait until she got back in the boat, then he'd make his move. He had it all planned. Every little detail. He would hail her, pretending to have engine trouble, and then when she offered him a ride—

A flare of bright light, followed by a loud *boom*,

caught him off guard, and then the force of the blast knocked him back a step or two.

As Jack watched in horror, Celeste's boat exploded in flames, and a moment later, the swell of water beneath the hull of his own boat pitched him forward. He had to grab on to the rail to keep from going overboard.

Bracing himself, he lifted the binoculars and stared at the spot in the water where he'd last seen her. He could find nothing now but bits of burning debris floating on the waves.

Sliding behind the wheel, he started the engine and turned the boat sharply, opening up the throttle as he headed for the flaming vessel. Circling the wreckage, he scanned the water, his heart like a drumbeat inside his chest. On his second pass around, he spotted her. She'd surfaced about fifty yards away, and when she saw him, she began to frantically hail him.

Easing back on the throttle, Jack brought the boat alongside her, then leaned over the edge to give her a hand up. She came slithering over the side like a frightened mermaid, all wet and slinky and golden.

If her breasts were smaller than he'd imagined, the rest of her was curvier. Not as lean and toned as in her movies, but sexy, nonetheless.

She wasn't as drop-dead gorgeous, either, without the makeup and subtle lighting. The harsh glare of sunlight revealed a smattering of freckles across her nose and highlighted an unsightly bruise on her upper

thigh. She wasn't flawless by any stretch of the imagination.

Was he disappointed? Jack wasn't sure. In some ways, it was a relief to know that she wasn't quite as perfect as the image he'd seen on the big screen. Because nobody could live up to that.

He knelt beside her. "Are you all right?"

"I…think so. I don't know what happened…" She lay in the bottom of the boat, not gracefully posed but with arms and legs sprawled all over the place.

Her breasts were barely hidden by her skimpy swimsuit top, and Jack tried to glance away. Honest. He did. But they were right *there*. Practically in his face. And he'd seen them, in all their glory, just moments ago.

Even though his sunglasses hid his eyes, she must have sensed the direction of his gaze because she quickly covered herself.

Gallantly, he whipped a shirt off the back of a seat and handed it to her. She accepted it gratefully, tugging it over her breasts and all the way down to her knees. Wrapping her arms around her legs, she sat trembling on the floor like a netted fish.

"Are you sure you're all right?" he asked again.

She swiped a wet strand of hair from her face. "Yes, but…I don't understand what…happened. One moment I was in the water…and the next thing I knew—" She broke off, her eyes going wide as she stared up at him.

Too late, Jack realized his cap had blown off during the rescue, revealing his shock of bleached hair.

She put fingertips to her lips. "You're…*him*," she said in wonder.

In a matter of seconds, Jack's carefully laid plans had literally gone up in smoke, but he was nothing if not resourceful. He could improvise with the best of them. "Him?" *Yeah, that was brilliant.*

"I saw you at Metro. You were—" Beneath the beginnings of a sunburn, her face turned an even brighter shade of red. "What are you doing here?" she asked still in that same tone of awe.

So she'd recognized him, but at least she didn't seem suspicious. That was a good sign, Jack decided. It gave him something to work with. "What am I doing here? I'm rescuing you. In case you didn't notice, your boat just exploded. Lucky I decided to go fishing today."

She pushed herself away from him as suspicion set in with a vengeance. "*Luck?* Are you telling me this is some sort of coincidence?"

He hesitated, then decided to go with plan B. "Not exactly—"

"Oh, God, I think I'm going to be sick." She crawled on all fours to the side of the boat. Then pulling herself up, she hung her head over the rail and retched noisily into the water until there was nothing left in her stomach.

Jack stood by helplessly, not quite certain what to

do. The sight of the woman upchucking over the side of the boat was in such extreme contradiction to the woman on the silver screen. He couldn't get over it.

But far from being repulsed, Jack had the utmost sympathy for her because he'd been in her position more than a few times. Usually by his own doing, but still…

He wet a towel in the water, then held it out to her as her dry heaves finally subsided. She collapsed weakly in the bottom of the boat, holding the towel to her face. "That must have been attractive."

Jack grinned. "Just consider it your contribution to the Gulf's ecological system. I'm sure the fish appreciate the effort."

"That's disgusting." But she looked grateful that he'd decided to make light of an awkward situation. "I guess it just hit me all at once…how close I came to…" She shuddered violently. "If I hadn't jumped in the water, I'd be dead right now."

Jack had been thinking about that, too.

"How could something like that happen?" She pressed the wet towel to her forehead as she gazed up at him. "How could a boat just explode like that?"

Jack shrugged. "Could have been a fuel leak." But he didn't really believe that. He glanced up and quickly scanned the water. Attracted by the explosion, several boats raced toward them. Jack turned and surreptitiously pulled a .38 from his

bag, then slipped it underneath a towel on the seat beside them.

The nearest boat, a maroon-and-white cabin cruiser similar to the one that had exploded, began to hail them. A moment later, the craft pulled alongside them. Jack kept his hand on the seat, mere inches from the .38.

"Anyone hurt?" a man called out.

"Everyone's fine," Jack said. "We think there may have been a fuel leak."

"Hell of an explosion," the newcomer observed. He had three passengers with him, two women and a man. They all gazed at the flaming wreckage in awe. "Anything we can do to help?"

"I've notified the coast guard," Jack said. "In the meantime, better not get too close."

The man nodded, then turning to say something to the others, he pulled away. Several boats were ringing the smoldering wreckage by now, but most of them had enough sense to keep a safe distance.

"We should get out of here, too," Jack said. "A stray gust of wind, and we could have a real disaster on our hands."

Celeste was still shivering as she gazed up at him. "Shouldn't we wait for the coast guard? You did radio them, right? You said you did."

"It's all taken care of. Don't worry," he said. "Right now, let's put some distance between us and that fire."

As he started to turn away, she scrambled to her feet. Struggling to keep her balance, she stared at him in wide-eyed fear. "I'm not going anywhere with you. Not until you tell me who you are and why you've been following me."

Yeah, genius. Tell her who you are and why you've been following her. I can't wait to hear this myself.

"Are you a reporter?" she asked suddenly.

He shook his head. "No, I'm a cop." Jack had never particularly subscribed to the honesty-is-the-best-policy approach, but he knew from his under-cover stints with HPD that a little truth could sometimes go a long way. At least that was his hope.

"A…cop?" Something that might have been guilt flickered in her eyes as her hand flew to her throat. It was a defensive gesture, but Jack had no idea why.

Interesting. It appeared Celeste Fortune had a few secrets of her own. "My name is Jack Fury. I work for…Interpol."

"Interpol?" She frowned in confusion. "But I thought…I thought Interpol was some kind of Euro-pean police agency."

"It is. But I was born and raised around here. I know the territory. That's why I was given the assign-ment."

"What kind of assignment?"

"For the past several months, we've been on the trail of a notorious jewel thief. We've followed him

all over Europe, and now we've reason to believe that he's here in the States. In Houston, to be exact, and we think he's set his sights on the Mirabelle Hotel." He was improvising his butt off, and getting himself in deeper and deeper by the minute.

Celeste gasped. "The Mirabelle? But that's where I'm—"

"Yes, I know."

The next few seconds were critical. She'd either accept him at his word, or start screaming bloody murder. It was to Jack's advantage not to allow her much time to consider the two choices. "That's why I've been following you," he hastened to add.

"But—" She bit her lip in confusion. "I don't understand. You don't think I'm somehow connected to this thief, do you?"

His gaze held hers. "No. I think you're his next target."

CASSIE STARED at him in shock. "*Me?* Why would a jewel thief target me? I don't have anything of value—" She broke off, realizing her gaffe. Cassie Boudreaux owned nothing of value, but Celeste Fortune had undoubtedly been showered with expensive gifts from her rich lover.

Jack Fury cocked his head. "Nothing of value? I wouldn't exactly call the Boucheron diamond worthless." When she said nothing, he smiled. "Yes, we know all about Owen Fleming's recent acquisition

from Sotheby's. When the stone didn't turn up on his wife's finger, we assumed he'd bought it for his mistress. You."

Was that censure in his tone? Cassie wondered. Or was she imagining his disapproval? She couldn't help feeling guilty about the affair even though she hadn't been one of the participants. But Jack didn't know that. He couldn't know that she was only culpable of impersonating her cousin, but that wasn't a crime, was it? *Was* it?

"As you can see, I'm not in possession of any rings," she managed to say coolly as she waved her hands in front of him.

"You'd hardly wear a rare ten-carat pink diamond to the beach, now would you? If you're smart, you've got it stashed someplace safe."

As she watched him, Cassie's suspicions suddenly returned. There was something about him… about his demeanor…about this whole setup…

Why had Celeste never mentioned the Boucheron diamond? Surely, a stone of such…epic proportions was something Cassie should have been made aware of, in case people asked questions. And by people, she meant Jack Fury.

She lifted her chin, prepared to improvise as best she could. "If you expect me to tell you where I keep my jewelry, you're in for a shock. You say you're a cop, but you haven't shown me any identification. For all I know, *you're* the jewel thief."

"I haven't shown you any identification because I'm undercover," he said. "I can't exactly go around flashing my ID and badge, now can I?"

Cassie's gaze narrowed. Again, his explanation was just a little too convenient. On the other hand, if he really was working undercover, that might explain the overprocessed hair.

Still, Cassie knew she'd be a fool to simply take him at his word. And yet…even as her doubts continued to mount, she couldn't help but remember the way he'd reacted at the restaurant to what they'd both thought was gunfire. He hadn't hesitated even for a moment to protect her. His response had been instinctive, just as a cop's would be.

Even now, his gaze on her was steady. Not shifting or wavering, but so relentless that Cassie felt a tremor course through her. His eyes were even bluer than she remembered. A deep ocean blue that made her wonder about hidden depths.

"Do you remember what happened at the restaurant the other night?" she asked reluctantly. "Almost everyone on the patio thought that sound was a gunshot. Did you?"

He shrugged. "I did at first."

"Is that why you dove for me?"

"Sure."

"But why would you assume I was the target? Why would a jewel thief want to kill me?"

His gaze left hers then to scan the ocean. "I didn't

stop to think about it. I just reacted because I didn't want you to get hurt."

Something in his voice made Cassie's heart start to pound even harder. Was it a note of sincerity? "Afterwards, I saw you on top of the building across the street. You were looking down at me."

His gaze met hers again. "I thought I saw someone up there. I went to check it out."

"And what about today? Why did you follow me to Galveston? If you think the jewel thief is after the—" What had he called it? "—Boucheron diamond, why didn't you stay back at the hotel and watch for him?"

"Because he knows you're too smart to entrust a three-million-dollar ring to a hotel safe. He also knows that a woman in love would want to keep an expensive gift from her lover somewhere close by."

"Who says I'm in love?" Cassie blurted.

Jack's gaze narrowed. "Aren't you?"

She pushed back her wet hair. "Owen and I are finished, haven't you heard?"

"Yes, I heard that."

"Then how do you know I didn't give the ring back?"

"Because you'd be a fool to give away that kind of security now that your career has—shall we say—suffered some setbacks."

There it was again, the barest hint of disapproval, and this time Cassie was a little annoyed by it.

"How is it you seem to know so much about me?" she demanded.

"I make it my business to know everything about the people involved in the cases I'm working. I don't like surprises."

Then brace yourself, mister.

But Cassie wasn't yet ready to come clean with Jack Fury. A part of her wanted to trust him because, after all, what was her alternative? Jump back into the water? They were too far out for her to swim to shore, and if she hailed another boat, how could she be certain she wasn't flagging down the real jewel thief? If he even existed.

But that wasn't the real reason Cassie kept silent. To be honest, there was something deeply thrilling about being the object of Jack Fury's attention. And once he found out she wasn't Celeste, she'd be about as interesting to him as yesterday's catch.

He was just so different from anyone Cassie had ever met before. She'd known there was something special about him the moment she'd set eyes on him at Metro. But she'd thought at first her attraction stemmed from the effortless way he blended into the arty world to which she'd always hoped to belong. Now she realized it was something else. Her thirst for adventure—for something *more*—drew her to him.

She'd been starved for life for far too long, and now Jack Fury, with a story as improbable as his hair color, promised her a feast.

Cassie thought back to that night at the restaurant, the little game they'd played with one another, and she shuddered.

The attraction was still there, no question about it. She just wasn't sure what to do about it.

Her mind raced with the possibilities. "What about the boat?"

"What about it?"

"Do you think your jewel thief had something to do with the explosion?"

He hesitated. "That's what I intend to find out."

He turned away from her then, and Cassie saw his hand snake out to grab something from underneath a towel on one of the seats. He was so quick about it that she had only a brief glimpse of something dark and metallic, but she knew instinctively that it was a gun.

So he was armed and, for all she knew, dangerous. And here she was alone with him on the high seas.

A measure of common sense returned. Adventure was one thing, but deliberately placing herself in imminent peril quite another.

What did she think she was doing? How could she even consider starting something up with Jack Fury? She knew nothing about the man. She didn't even know if he was a real cop. What if he'd made up the whole Interpol-jewel thief story? What if, instead, he was some kind of…stalker?

Maybe he'd blown up the boat, just so he could rescue her. Get close to her.

Cassie had seen a similar scenario in a movie once. A psycho who'd set up all kinds of bizarre situations just so he could be near the object of his fascination.

Jack Fury might be a little on the strange side, but to be fair, he hadn't done anything truly psychotic. Although Cassie was pretty sure he'd been staring at her breasts earlier, but she could hardly blame him for that. Her new Brazilian swimsuit was pretty skimpy, and truthfully, she might have been a little disappointed if he hadn't snuck a peek.

Still, why had he told the man in the other boat that he'd called the coast guard when he obviously hadn't?

Unless…he hadn't wanted the others to call…

Because…he had something to hide…

Come to think of it, Cassie wasn't all that keen on involving the authorities, either. Ethan Gold had made arrangements for Celeste to have the use of his boat, but Cassie wasn't Celeste. Technically, she'd taken it out without Professor Gold's permission, which meant that if he pressed charges, she could end up in jail. Or be forced to cough up the dough to reimburse him for damages. In either case, she'd be in deep doo-doo.

But back to Jack Fury…

He didn't appear crazy or perverted, thank goodness. Then again, neither, apparently, had Ted Bundy.

But try as she might, Cassie just couldn't picture a psycho killer in a pair of lime-green board shorts.

She couldn't exactly picture an Interpol agent in a getup like that, either, but that didn't stop her from appreciating the way those shorts hugged his lean hips and accentuated the ripple of subtle muscle in his abs and chest. The way they rode so low that with just a little tug…

What in the world had gotten into her? She'd just destroyed someone's boat, barely escaped with her life, and now here she was, moments later, lusting after the guy who'd pulled her out of the water.

A guy who claimed to be an Interpol agent on the trail of an international jewel thief.

If Cassie bought that, he probably had a nice little bridge in Brooklyn he'd like to sell her, too.

Chapter Seven

A few minutes later they were back at the marina, and Cassie hopped out of the boat to help Jack tie off. "What do we do now?" she asked anxiously.

Jack grabbed a nylon bag from one of the seats and dug around for his cell phone. "I've got a buddy who works for the Galveston Police Department. I'll see if I can track him down and get him over here."

"What about the coast guard?"

"The coast guard knows how to reach me. Right now I want to talk to the locals first."

After he made the call, they walked to a seaside restaurant near the marina to wait, and Jack guided her to a booth near the back. He took the seat facing the door and ordered coffee for both of them. They talked quietly until his friend arrived a short while later.

"There's Vargas," Jack said as he spotted the cop at the door. He slid out of the booth. "Excuse me for a minute. I want to fill him in on what's going on."

Or warn him not to say too much, Cassie thought uneasily. She turned and watched Jack stride to the front of the restaurant. The man he spoke to looked to be in his midthirties, dark hair, dark eyes, and the kind of good-humored expression that made you instantly like him.

He glanced toward the back of the restaurant, and when his gaze met Cassie's, recognition and something she couldn't name sparked in his black eyes before he turned back to Jack.

They conferred for a few minutes longer before joining Cassie. Jack made the introductions. "This is Sergeant Vargas with the Galveston PD. Celeste Fortune."

Vargas nodded and reached to shake Cassie's hand. "It's a pleasure to meet you, Miss Fortune. Jack's told me a lot about you."

Her brows lifted in surprise. "He has? Just now?"

Vargas grinned. "He's a real fast talker, our Jack." He clapped Jack's shoulder. "Mind if I have a minute alone with Miss Fortune?"

Jack frowned. "Is that really necessary?"

"I think so."

Jack hesitated, obviously displeased by the sergeant's suggestion, then he shrugged and backed off.

Vargas waited until Jack was out of earshot, then he took the seat across from Cassie. "Jack tells me you ran into a little trouble today. Care to tell me what happened?"

Nervously, Cassie toyed with her cup. "I'll tell you what I know, which isn't much. But first…I wonder if I could ask you something."

When the waitress brought Vargas over a cup of coffee, he thanked her politely, then immediately refocused his attention on Cassie as he stirred a packet of sweetener into the liquid. "What is it?"

"Could I see some identification?"

He looked surprised by the request, but he obligingly hauled out his badge and ID and allowed Cassie to scrutinize his credentials.

Satisfied that he really was a cop, she glanced up with an apologetic smile. "I'm sorry. It's just…I don't really know Jack Fury very well. I only have his word that he's who he says he is. Unlike you, he wasn't willing to show me any identification, but I take it you know him? You can vouch for him?"

"Jack?" Vargas took a careful sip of his coffee and grimaced. "We go way back. Worked a case together five years ago and we've been buddies ever since."

"Then he really is a cop?"

His gaze met Cassie's over the rim of his cup. "He was one of the best when I worked with him."

She sat back in relief. "That's good to know. All that business about an international jewel thief…Interpol…I didn't quite know what to believe."

Vargas's expression turned sober. "Here's what you can believe, Miss Fortune. If Jack Fury thinks you're in danger, you'd better listen up. He has the

best instincts of any cop I ever knew. His investigative techniques may be a little unorthodox, but I learned a long time ago there's usually a method to his madness. And as for his integrity…I'd trust him with my life."

He sounded so sincere, Cassie couldn't help but believe him. She nodded gratefully. "Thanks."

"Now let's get back to you," Vargas said briskly. "Tell me what happened today."

"There isn't much I can add to what Jack told you on the phone. The boat I took out earlier exploded in the Gulf. I don't know how or why. All I know is that one minute everything seemed fine, and the next thing I knew, it was in flames."

"You were in the water at the time?"

"Yes, I…" She glanced down. "I dropped something in the water and I jumped in to get it. That's when it happened."

"Lucky timing." Vargas stirred another packet of sweetener into his coffee. "The boat is registered in your name?"

"No. It belongs to a man named Ethan Gold. But I had his permission to use it," she rushed to assure him. "I'm staying in his beach house this weekend."

"Where can I reach Mr. Gold?"

"It's Professor Gold. He teaches drama at the University of Houston. But I'm…not sure where he is at the moment." Cassie was treading in dangerous water. She had to be careful because if she admitted

who she was, all sorts of questions would ensue. And possibly a few legal entanglements as well. She might even be thrown in jail until her cousin surfaced to vouch for her.

If she surfaced. Cassie was no longer certain that she could count on Celeste to bail her out of trouble. Truth be told, she was no longer certain of anything. What had started out as a harmless charade had suddenly turned very deadly, and Cassie didn't know what to do. Who to trust. But until she had a chance to think things through, maybe even confer with an attorney, self-preservation told her to keep her mouth shut.

"Professor Gold is out of town this weekend," she explained. "I don't know where he is."

"Do you have his home address?"

"Not with me. I'm sure I have it somewhere back at my hotel. I think he lives in the West University area."

He glanced up. "You think? You don't know?"

Cassie tried to shrug casually. "We're not that close. He was my drama professor years ago. We've kept in touch sporadically through phone calls and letters, but I haven't actually seen him in quite some time."

"But he offered you the use of his beach house and boat. Sounds to me as if you two are still pretty close."

"Not really. He's…a very generous man." Cassie had no idea if Vargas believed her or not. She could read nothing from his expression.

Very deliberately, he stirred even more sweetener into his coffee. "Did he ever mention any trouble he might be in?"

"What do you mean?"

"Do you know anyone who might want him dead?" Vargas said bluntly.

Cassie gasped. "Dead?"

"Boats don't just explode for no reason, Miss Fortune. If Professor Gold wasn't the target, then we have to assume that—"

She was. Or, more accurately, Celeste. A shudder ripped up Cassie's spine. She had the sudden urge to tell Vargas everything, but the fear of repercussions—namely, jail—held her back.

"Is there anyone who would want to harm you, Miss Fortune?"

"I…don't know."

His gaze darkened as he leaned toward her. "If I were you, I'd give the question a great deal of thought. Like I said, boats don't just explode." He scooted out of the booth and stood. "In the meantime, I'll need the professor's address and phone number. Have Jack give me a call when you get back to your hotel."

Cassie glanced up. "That's it? That's all you need from me?"

His gaze bore into hers. "Unless you have something more to tell me."

"Uh, no, I've told you everything I know," Cassie said nervously. Even though his expression re-

mained neutral, she had a feeling he could see right through her.

But all he said was, "I'll be in touch."

Cassie turned to watch him leave. Just outside the door of the restaurant, he stopped to have a word with Jack who had changed from his swim trunks into jeans and a casual shirt. He and Sergeant Vargas conversed for several minutes, then Vargas disappeared and Jack entered the restaurant.

Cassie turned quickly and pretended she hadn't been watching them. When Jack approached the table, she made a point of staring out the window.

"Ready to go?"

She turned. "Go where?"

He shrugged. "Back to Houston, I guess. I'll give you a lift. You still look too shaky to drive."

"But I have a rental car…and the keys were in my bag on the boat." Along with her driver's license and some spare cash. Without money or wheels, Cassie would have no way of getting back to the hotel. Unless she called one of the Cantrells to come get her, and hell would freeze over before she'd do that.

There was nothing to do but accept Jack's offer.

"You can call the rental company from the hotel," he said as she slid out of the booth.

He took her elbow as they left the restaurant, and in spite of the warning bells he set off, Cassie shivered at his touch.

"I CAN'T GO BACK to Houston yet," she said as they walked to a public parking lot near the marina. "I have to fetch Mr. Bogart."

"Who's Mr. Bogart?"

"He's a dog. A Chihuahua. My Chihuahua. He's my...Chihuahua," Cassie finished lamely.

Jack gave her a curious glance. "Yeah, I got that." He pointed to a late-model sedan, then used the remote to unlock the doors. The car wasn't at all what Cassie had expected, but perhaps the nondescript vehicle was part of his cover.

He opened the door for her, then went around to slide behind the wheel. "Where do we find Mr. Bogart?"

"He's at Professor Gold's beach house."

Cassie gave Jack directions, and as they drove along the coastal roadway, she studied him covertly from the corner of her eye.

Did she trust him?

In spite of Sergeant Vargas's ringing endorsement, she still hadn't decided. The idea that Jack had been following her—maybe for days—left her distinctly uncomfortable. He'd seen her in unguarded moments, and that alone was enough to make her shy away from him.

And then there was that little scene at Metro.

The two of them had practically been making out in public. Cassie could only imagine what he must think of her after that...unseemly display.

He turned, saw her staring, and smiled.

And, boy, what a smile. The way his lips tilted slightly at the corners made Cassie think all kinds of things she had no business thinking, especially in light of the fact that she'd almost been shark bait little more than an hour ago. Talk about unseemly.

But…she'd been yearning for an adventure, and now here she was, smack-dab in the middle of a doozy.

"Which way?" Jack asked as they came to an intersection.

"Left."

He made the turn, and as they drove along the narrow lane, Cassie noticed two twenty-something women in thong bikinis admiring a silver Jaguar parked on the side of the road. Cassie wasn't sure why, but as she and Jack drove by, she turned to glance back. One of the girls lifted a cell phone to her ear and said something into the mouthpiece as she stared after Cassie and Jack.

There was nothing unusual in the girl's action, Cassie told herself. Young women talked on cell phones all the time.

She put the incident out of her mind as Jack pulled into Ethan Gold's driveway. "I won't be long," she told him, "but you're welcome to come in if you want."

"I'll wait on the landing." They both got out of the car, and Jack followed her up the stairs.

At the top, Cassie fished a key from underneath

a flowerpot and opened the front door. She took a step inside, then froze.

The room had been totally trashed. Paintings and cushions had been ripped to shreds, furniture overturned, lamps smashed. Even the carpet had been slashed.

Cassie hadn't consciously made a noise, but she must have cried out in dismay because suddenly Jack was right behind her. When he put a hand on her arm, she started violently. He said in her ear, "Wait here."

He pulled a gun from the back waistband of his jeans—which had been hidden by his shirt—and slowly walked into the room. Flattening himself against the wall, he eased toward the hallway. Glancing back at Cassie, he put a finger to his lips, cautioning her to silence, then he turned and peered around the corner. Finding the coast clear, he disappeared down the corridor.

He'd been gone for only a few seconds when Cassie heard an engine rev somewhere below her. Instinctively, she started down the stairs, but before she made it to the bottom, Jack rushed past her, shoving her aside in his haste.

"He went out the back!" he yelled as he raced to the sedan and jumped in. But just as he reversed out of the drive, a car across the street backed out and blocked him.

Jack laid on the horn, but the noise seemed to

only confuse the other driver. The car stopped just inches from the sedan's bumper and remained there.

Infuriated, Jack jumped out of the car and waved for the driver to move. The car didn't budge.

By this time, Cassie had made it down the stairs and into the driveway. She glanced down the street in time to see the silver Jaguar take off like a bullet. The driver made the intersection without stopping, then vanished down the street.

Jack ran over to the other car, but before he reached the driver's window, the vehicle shot forward and he had to jump out of the way.

As the car sped away, Cassie caught a glimpse of the driver. The windows were tinted, but she was pretty sure the girl behind the wheel was the same one who had been talking on the cell phone earlier.

Cassie hurried down the driveway toward Jack. "Aren't you going to chase them?"

"Do you really think I could catch a Jag in that thing?" He nodded toward the sedan.

"You think that girl deliberately backed out in front of you?"

"It looked pretty damn deliberate to me," Jack said grimly. "She must have used her cell phone to warn him we were coming. But at least I got the plate numbers on both vehicles."

Cassie hadn't even thought of that. Everything had happened too quickly. She caught Jack's arm. "Who do you think was in there? Did you see him?"

He ran a hand through his blond hair. "I didn't get a good look. The back door was open, and by the time I spotted him, he was making a beeline for the Jag."

"Are you sure it was a he?"

Jack glanced down at her in surprise. "Why? Do you have someone in mind?"

Cassie bit her lip. "No, not really." But she couldn't help thinking that the wanton destruction inside the beach house might have been the act of a scorned woman. Or a scorned woman's hired minions.

Jack took out his cell phone. "I'd better get Vargas over here to file a report. Gold's insurance company is going to be pissed. First his boat, and now this."

And more than likely, Cassie was going to catch heat for both incidents. She was getting in more deeply by the minute, but instead of coming clean, she held her tongue and watched Jack make the call. Then they both went back upstairs.

"Don't touch anything," he warned as she started to go inside.

"I won't. But I have to find Mr. Bogart. He's probably scared half to death."

"All right, go ahead," Jack muttered. "I doubt very seriously whoever did this left prints. He knew what he was doing."

Or she. Cassie wasn't yet ready to rule out Margo Fleming's culpability in the day's events. Hadn't

Mrs. Ambrose-Pritchard warned her of what the woman might be capable?

Cassie left Jack in the living room to go find Mr. Bogart. But after a few minutes of fruitless searching, she started to panic. What if Margo or her henchmen had done something to him? What better revenge against Celeste? Everyone knew how much she loved that little dog. If any harm had come to him, how would Cassie break it to her cousin?

She realized with something of a shock that she'd take the loss pretty hard herself. She wasn't a dog person—never had been. But she had to admit that Mr. Bogart, with his beady little eyes and temperamental disposition, had found his way into her heart.

"Please," she whispered. "Just let me find you safe and sound. I'll never scold you again. I'll give you all the doggie treats you can eat, and take you for long walks in the park. You can stop at every tree if you want. I'll even put in a good word with Chablis's mommy. Come on, Bogey. Just tell me where you are. Give me some kind of sign."

Cassie was just about to give up when she heard a whimper coming from the bathroom. The door was closed so she used the tail of her shirt—or rather Jack's shirt, which she still wore over her swimsuit—to turn the knob.

Shoving the door open with her toe, she peered

inside. The whimpers came from behind the shower curtain, and a more pitiful sound Cassie had never heard. She had no idea what the intruder might have done to the poor little pooch, but her imagination was very good at conjuring up the worst.

Steeling herself, she crossed the room and yanked back the curtain.

And there he sat, quivering in the bathtub, apparently unharmed except for his dignity. Cassie knew that feeling only too well. She sprung him from his porcelain prison, and cuddled him close as she carried him down the hallway.

Still trembling, he buried his head under her arm and he didn't come out until he heard Jack's voice. Then his head shot out and his ears pricked up. Spying Jack in the living room, he squirmed out of Cassie's grasp and ran over to sniff his leg. He sat down and began to wag his tail furiously.

"I've never seen him do that," Cassie said in awe. "He doesn't usually like strangers." The dog had never even seen Jack before, but there he was, acting as if the cop was his long lost friend.

Jack reached down and gave him a quick scratch behind the ears. "Wish you could tell me who did this, buddy."

The little dog yapped shrilly as if he were, indeed, trying to tell them something. Then he turned and raced back down the hallway.

Exchanging a puzzled glance, Jack and Cassie

followed him. He ran into the bathroom and began to paw frantically at something on the tile floor.

"What do you think he's doing?" Cassie said from the doorway.

Jack brushed by her and squatted to get a closer look. "I think he's found some blood."

"Blood?" Cassie was appalled. "Then they did do something to him."

"I'd say it was the other way around. I think Mr. Bogart probably put up quite a fight, and what we have here is the suspect's DNA."

Cassie glanced down at the dog. "Really? He did that?"

"Poor devil probably didn't even realize he was bleeding. Good work, Bogey." Jack scratched behind the dog's ears again, and the Chihuahua positively strutted from the room.

So Jack Fury had a way with animals. *Interesting.* Cassie wondered suddenly how he was with kids.

VARGAS ARRIVED fifteen minutes later with a couple of uniformed officers. While they dusted for prints, he filled out the paperwork and took statements. By the time they'd finished, the sun was setting, and Cassie was happy to see the end of a very dark day.

She hurriedly dressed in jeans and a T-shirt and gathered up her weekend bag. She couldn't wait to put distance between herself and the beach. What had started off as a promising weekend had ended in

disaster, and now all she wanted was a long soak in her own private Jacuzzi back at the Mirabelle.

She knew she had a lot to mull over, plans to make, consequences to consider, but right now she was too exhausted to even think straight.

Only after they'd crossed the causeway and were headed back to Houston did she breathe a sigh of relief. As the tension began to drain away, she even managed to doze off, but she awakened with a start when she felt the car slow.

She opened her eyes, expecting to find that they were back in the city, but instead they were cruising along the feeder road of I-45.

When Jack made a turn, Cassie bolted up in alarm. "What are you doing? Where are you taking me? What's going on?"

Jack shot her a glance. "I'm taking you someplace where we can talk in private."

"We can't do that back at the hotel?"

"This can't wait."

Cassie shivered at his tone. "What do you want to talk about?"

"Do you even have to ask? The boat you took out blew up, and someone ransacked the house you were staying in. I'd say we have a lot to talk about."

Suddenly, the tension was back, throbbing at Cassie's temples. She tried to massage away the stabbing pain. "Do you think whoever trashed Professor Gold's beach house was after the diamond?"

"Maybe." Jack glanced in the rearview mirror as if to make sure they weren't being followed. His action only added to Cassie's unease, and she turned to glance over her shoulder.

"But why blow up the boat? He couldn't have known I didn't have the ring with me. For all he knew, he could have sent the diamond to the bottom of the ocean along with me." Cassie turned suddenly. "Jack, what if the two incidents aren't related? What if the jewel thief is after the diamond, and someone else is after…me?"

"I've thought of that possibility," he admitted. "At this point, I don't think we can rule out anything."

"But if you're on the trail of the jewel thief, you can't afford to be sidetracked by…whatever else is going on," Cassie said. "Can you?"

He shrugged. "Don't worry about that. I follow the clues wherever they lead me."

Ookay. Cassie drew a long breath. Jack's answer was evasive at best, but suddenly she didn't care. She still wasn't sure she trusted him, but she knew she felt safer with him around.

She also knew from the experience at Metro that he would protect her, even with his own life if need be, and that realization was a great comfort to her.

And a powerful aphrodisiac. Not that she needed much encouragement. At least where Jack Fury was concerned, anyway.

Cassie's gaze swept over him. If he had been fol-

lowing her for days, how could she not have noticed him? There was just something about him. He wasn't conventionally handsome by any stretch of the imagination, but Cassie had a feeling that he was a veritable chick magnet. The impossible hair color only added to his appeal because it gave him an edge. And a sense of humor. She didn't think a guy with hair like that could possibly take himself too seriously, although she sensed he was deadly serious about his job.

The light-colored hair brought out the deep blue of his eyes and contrasted nicely with his dark, thick lashes. And those lips…*mama mia,* those lips…

Cassie could fantasize about those lips for hours. She could write poems about those lips. Daydream about having them whisper along her throat, nuzzle the hollow between her breasts, and then, if she was lucky, he'd keep right on going.

As she got a little carried away with the fantasy, Cassie squirmed in her seat, realizing that her nipples had gone quite hard beneath the thin fabric of her T-shirt. Jack pretended not to notice, but Cassie had a feeling very little escaped his attention.

Chapter Eight

Ho…ly…

Jack cut himself off in midthought. He was trying to clean up his language, not to mention his mind, but it wasn't easy with Celeste Fortune around. The woman was hot.

How had he ever thought she didn't measure up to her screen image? Film just did not do her justice. There she sat, with limp hair and a sunburned face, and Jack didn't think she'd ever looked sexier.

He could see the outline of her breasts through her thin T-shirt, and the nipple action she had going was enough to send his blood pressure through the roof. He could feel himself getting aroused just watching her, and he tried to avert his gaze, but *he'd seen those breasts before*. He didn't have to use his imagination. He knew what they looked like, and all that was left to do know now was touch them, taste them…

She'd probably slap his face if he got out of line, and Jack wouldn't blame her a bit. He admired a

woman who wasn't afraid to stand up for herself, but at the same time, there was that tiny spark in her eyes that suggested she just might not be all that opposed to his advances.

Take it easy. She was just a job, and if he had any sense, he'd keep their relationship on a purely professional basis. He had enough to worry about right now. Like who was out to get her.

Someone had blown up that boat, trashed the beach house and the suspect might well be the person he'd seen the other night trying to break into her hotel suite. The perp appeared to be getting bolder and more desperate by the day, and Jack knew from experience that desperation was a very dangerous commodity.

As he pulled into the gravel parking lot of a restaurant named Pop's, he flashed Celeste another glance. She was staring out the window, but sensing his perusal, she turned to face him. His gaze dropped in spite of himself, but he recovered so quickly he hoped she hadn't noticed.

She crossed her arms over her breasts. Oh, she'd noticed, all right. "I don't think this is such a good idea," she said. "I can't leave Mr. Bogart in here. It's too hot."

"I've got some pull with the owners. There's a shady little courtyard around back where we can put him. He can stretch his legs while we talk. Just give me a minute to set up everything." Jack left the

engine and air conditioner running as he got out of the car.

Striding across the parking lot, he glanced around. The place looked abandoned. The outside of the building appeared to have been cobbled together from weathered planks, license plates, and rusted signs, but looks could be deceiving, as he knew only too well.

Inside, some of the best seafood and burgers in the area were served while fifties tunes blasted from the jukebox. Later, when more people headed back to Houston after a long day at the beach, the restaurant would fill up and overflow onto the picnic tables scattered about the yard.

Pop's had been around for as long as Jack could remember, and he'd spent many a summer there busing tables and washing dishes before going off to college in Austin. After that, he'd found easier and more profitable ways of making some spare change.

Taking the porch steps two at a time, he opened the door and stood just inside for a moment, letting the familiar sights and smells wrap around him like an old worn blanket. Pop was behind the bar watching an Astros game on TV while his wife Betty placed fresh daisies from her garden in bud vases on the Formica tables.

She glanced up momentarily when she heard the door, then did a double take. "Jackie? Is that you? Stu, look who it is!" She hurried toward the door. "It's Jackie!"

Stu Fury tore himself from the game and glanced around. When he saw Jack, his mouth gaped in astonishment. "…the hell?"

"Hello to you, too, Pop," Jack said with a grin. His stepmother enveloped him in a giant bear hug and for several long seconds, Jack could hardly breathe let alone speak. She was a petite woman, but she'd always been freakishly strong.

Even on the threshold of sixty, she remained thin, toned and tanned, but the way she dressed—like a hooker with very bad taste—did nothing to enhance her looks. She should have lost the miniskirts and short shorts thirty years ago, not to mention the platinum hair, but Jack wasn't exactly in any position to criticize, he decided as he caught a glimpse of his own hair in the long mirror behind the bar.

Besides, giving his stepmother fashion advice was pretty much the equivalent of a death wish. He'd left home a long time ago, but he still knew better than to cross Betty Fury. She could live up to her name, and then some.

She had Stu's number, too, but he'd never admit it. After nearly twenty years of marriage, he still tried to pretend he wore the pants in the family even though he, and everyone else, knew better.

They were as different as night and day, but somehow, to Jack's amazement, their relationship worked. Betty had been a twice-divorced cocktail waitress and Stu, a widower with three rowdy boys to raise

and a struggling business to run when the two of them had hooked up. Jack could still remember the day she moved in. She'd shown up at the restaurant with a suitcase in each hand and decked out in her finest hoochie-mama outfit.

Jack had been outraged at the thought of his father taking up with such a woman. Or *any* woman, really, because no one could possibly live up to the memories of his mother. He and his brothers had immediately set about to run off Pop's new wife, but they'd soon learned that a riled-up Betty Fury was not someone with whom they wanted to tangle.

They'd also learned that all that ferocity could just as quickly be turned on the poor, unfortunate soul who decided to pick on her stepsons. Betty was nothing if not loyal, and Jack had come to appreciate that trait more than any other over the years. She'd always been someone he could count on, and that meant a lot. He couldn't imagine now having grown up without her.

He hugged her back, then held her at arm's length and gave her a long appraisal. "You've had something done."

She swatted his hand. "You know better than that. The only way I'd go under the knife is on a mortician's table. And even then, he better be careful with the face." She patted her cheeks.

"Well, you've done something," Jack insisted. "Because you look ten, no twenty years younger

than the last time I saw you. You sure you didn't have a little nip and tuck?"

"I'll nip and tuck you," she warned, "if you keep up that nonsense. Now go on over and say hello to your daddy. It's high time you showed your face around here. You don't call, you don't come by. We've been worried about you, Jackie."

"I'm fine."

Stu grunted as Jack stepped up to the bar. "You don't look fine. You look like a damn fool with that hair."

"Now, Stu, leave him alone," Betty scolded. "I like his hair."

"You would," Stu grumbled. His gaze narrowed. "Don't tell me you've taken to the streets since you lost your job. You're not one of those—what do they call them?—man-whores, are you?"

"Stu, for heaven's sakes!" Betty said in outrage. "Men have every right to color their hair if they want. Some of them even wear makeup nowadays and get manicures and facials. Metrosexuals, they call them. I've always thought you boys could stand to get in tune with your feminine sides a little more—"

"For the love of God, woman, do you hear what you're saying?" Stu gave Jack a resigned look. "We have Oprah to thank for all that touchy-feely crap."

"I don't need Oprah to tell me how to think," Betty informed him. "I have a mind of my own, thank you very much—"

"Look," Jack cut in, knowing the two of them could go at it for hours. "I'm working undercover. That's why I colored my hair, and that's why I'm here. I need you to help me out."

Betty was instantly intrigued, but Stu looked suspicious. "Undercover? I thought you got your ass fired."

"I'm not working for the police department," Jack explained. "I've got a job with a private detective firm."

Betty squealed in delight. "You mean like Magnum? Or Rockford? Oh, I just adore James Garner—"

"Woman, zip it."

"Stu Fury, don't you dare speak to me in that tone of voice—"

"Are you two going to help me out or not?" Jack said impatiently.

"Of course, we'll help." Betty gave Stu a warning looking. "Just tell us what to do."

"You don't have to do anything," Jack said. "I've got a client out in the car. We need a quiet place to talk, so I'm going to bring her in here for a drink. But I don't want any interruptions, and I don't want you asking her a lot of questions. Got it?"

Betty nodded. "Sure, Jackie, but can I ask you something?"

He shrugged.

"Is she your girl?"

Jack's mind instantly flashed back to Celeste's breasts pressed against her shirtfront. Girl? She was all woman.

"Are you deaf?" Stu said. "He just said she was a client."

Betty didn't miss a beat. "I know what he *said,* Stu, but men often say one thing and mean quite another. Take you, for instance. You always pretend to be so cold and unfeeling, but in bed, you're a regular tiger—"

"Okay, I don't need to hear that," Jack said, and he sure as hell didn't want the mental image or else he might just have to gouge out his mental eyes. "I'm going to bring her in and I expect you both to be on your best behavior. Oh, and one more thing." He slid off the barstool. "She has a dog. All right if we put him in the courtyard?"

"Why, sure it is. The place seems so empty now that my little Phoebe's passed on." Betty sniffed. "Be nice to see a dog enjoying my garden again. Won't it, Stu?"

He grunted.

"What kind of dog is it?" Betty asked.

"A Chihuahua."

Stu snorted this time before he turned back to the game. Betty patted Jack's hand and said conspiratorially, "Don't mind him. He's happy to see you. He just doesn't like to show it."

Jack shrugged. "I'm cool with that."

Betty nodded. "You always were. I've never known

a boy so self-possessed. Or one who tried to be. You're just like Stu. You don't like to show your feelings, and you sure don't like the idea of needing someone. I can understand that after what happened to your mama, I guess, but I sometimes think Stu would be happier puttering around this place all by himself."

"Don't kid yourself," Jack said. "He'd be lost without you. He's just never going to admit it."

"I'm cool with that." The two of them shared another smile before Jack turned and left the restaurant.

As he went out the door, he heard his father say, "What the hell do you think he's up to?"

"Oh, Stu, stop fretting. You know he's a good boy. They all are."

"Thanks to you," Stu said gruffly.

Jack glanced over his shoulder just as the two of them shared a kiss, and something tightened inside his chest. He wondered, suddenly, if Betty was right. Maybe he wasn't quite as self-sufficient as he liked to think.

JACK OPENED the door and stuck his head inside the air-conditioned car. "Everything's all set." Reaching in, he shut off the engine, pocketed the key, then grabbed Mr. Bogart's leash. "Come on, boy. I'll show you where you can kick back and relax while Celeste and I have a little chat."

"Are you sure he'll be safe out here?" Cassie asked worriedly as she followed him to the back

gate. As they walked through to the courtyard, she glanced around in amazement. Apparently, the place was not only safe but a veritable paradise, complete with dappled sunlight and a sparkling waterfall. The fence was lined with oleander and jasmine, and Spanish moss dripped from the gnarled branches of a water oak.

"This place is incredible," Cassie breathed as she reached down and unclipped Mr. Bogart's leash from his collar. For a moment, he didn't move a muscle. He'd been cooped up for so long in the hotel room and beach house that he didn't quite know what to do with his first taste of freedom.

Then he went over and sat down tentatively next to a tiny pond. His tail began to twitch as he tracked goldfish through a maze of river rock, water lilies and maidenhair fern.

"Can't we stay out here, too?" Cassie wondered aloud.

"Let's get a drink first," Jack suggested. Carefully, he fastened the gate, then lead her into the restaurant.

They chose a booth by the windows, and no sooner were they seated than a platinum-haired waitress approached their table. She was dressed in one of the most outlandish getups Cassie had ever seen on a woman of her age, but rather than being offended by a customer's frank stare, the woman smiled warmly.

And Cassie took to her immediately. The woman didn't look a thing like her mother, but there was something about her genuine manner and kind nature that reminded Cassie of Felicity Boudreaux. She was surprised to find that for the first time in a long time, she didn't tear up when she thought about her mother.

"My name is Betty," the woman said as she bent to straighten the silverware. "I'll be your server today. What can I get you to drink?"

Her tone was surprisingly formal considering her attire, and she looked a little nervous, Cassie thought.

Jack said, "Celeste, I'd like you to meet my stepmother, Betty Fury. This is Celeste Fortune."

Betty looked crestfallen. "I thought you said you were working undercover. I was going to pretend I didn't know you."

"Miss Fortune already knows who I am."

"Oh." Betty hesitated. "She knows…everything?"

She and Jack exchanged glances, and Jack said quickly, "About my work with Interpol? Yes, she does."

"Inter—?"

"I'll have a glass of iced tea," he said quickly. "How about you?" He glanced at Cassie. "I can highly recommend Pop's margaritas."

"Speaking of Pop…" Betty turned and called over her shoulder, "Stu? Get over here. There's someone I want you to meet."

The man at the bar reluctantly tore his attention from the game and lumbered over to the booth. He looked to be around sixty, tall and beefy with sunburned skin, thick, white hair and blue eyes that reminded Cassie of Jack's.

Betty linked her arm through his and drew him forward. "This is Jack's friend Celeste Fortune. She knows all about his work with…Interpol." Her eyes twinkled as she glanced at Jack.

Stu merely scowled.

"Celeste would like to try one of your margaritas, Pop."

"They come highly recommended," Cassie said. She reached out to shake the man's hand.

His grip was very firm, and he looked her right in the eyes when he said, "Watch out for that boy of mine. He's a real slick talker. Always has been."

A tiny thrill shot up Cassie's backbone. From any other father, she would have thought that such a remark was spoken in jest, but there was nothing in Stu Fury's eyes but a gleam of steel. Cassie had a feeling he was a straight shooter, a straight talker, and in spite of his gruff demeanor, she liked him. And trusted him.

"I will," she murmured, and he nodded in satisfaction.

Now it was Jack who frowned. "How about that margarita?"

"Coming right up," Betty said brightly. "Come on,

Stu." She tugged on her husband's arm. "Let's give these kids a chance to talk."

The glance that Stu shot Jack before he turned and strode back to the bar could only be interpreted as a warning look. A few minutes later, Betty returned with the drinks. As she placed them on the table, she leaned in and said softly to Cassie, "Don't pay Stu any mind. He likes to give Jackie a hard time, but he's crazy about that kid. We all are."

Betty straightened and patted Jack's shoulder before turning to join her husband at the bar. Stu appeared to be engrossed in the ball game once again, but Cassie could tell that Betty was giving him an earful.

She glanced at Jack. "I like your folks."

"They have their moments." He picked up his tea, eyeing Cassie over the rim of the glass. "What about your family?"

"I don't see much of them. I more or less cut my ties when I moved to L.A." Cassie had always suspected that Celeste was embarrassed by her humble roots, and had been only too happy to leave her past behind her. That was why Cassie had been so surprised when Celeste had called out of the blue, and even more surprised to learn that she'd seen Cassie's engagement picture. She wondered now how Celeste had come by it because she seriously doubted her cousin subscribed to the *Manville Gazette*.

She sipped her drink. "Hmm, you're right. This is a great margarita."

Jack nodded absently. Shoving his own glass aside, he folded his arms on the table. "Who has it in for you, Celeste?"

His directness sent another shiver up Cassie's spine. "I don't know. Maybe someone has it in for Professor Gold, and I just got in the way."

Jack frowned. "Do you really believe that?"

Cassie shrugged. "I'd like to."

"What exactly is your relationship with Gold?"

"Like I told you earlier, we kept in touch after I moved to L.A., but there really isn't a relationship."

"But there used to be." His blue gaze drilled into hers.

Cassie said reluctantly, "We lived together for a while before I moved to L.A." For some reason, she didn't want to admit her cousin's past indiscretions to Jack. She didn't want him to think ill of Celeste, and by proxy, her.

"How did he take it when you left?"

"What do you mean?"

Jack glanced up. "His young, beautiful protégée deserting him for greener pastures. That had to hurt."

Cassie quickly averted her gaze before she gave herself away. Did he really think she was beautiful?

Or was that compliment based solely on Celeste's screen image?

"You think he could still be nursing a grudge?" she asked doubtfully.

"I've seen it before. Besides Gold, who knew you'd be at his beach house this weekend? Or on his boat?"

Cassie thought for a moment. "No one that I know of, except for my cousin—" Too late, she realized her mistake and stopped just short of giving herself away.

"Your cousin?"

She flicked salt from the rim of her glass. "My cousin…Cassie. We spoke recently."

"I thought you said you'd cut yourself off from your family."

Was that suspicion she heard in his voice? Cassie drew a breath. This was getting tricky. "I did. But like I said, Cassie and I spoke recently. I may have told her about the beach house and the boat."

"Is it possible she could have followed you there? Does she know anything about explosives—"

Cassie gasped. "What? No, of course not. And even if she did, she'd never try to hurt me. Why would she?"

His gaze flicked over her. "Look at you. You're a gorgeous woman in a glamorous profession. You think that's not going to create some jealousy and re-sentment in the people you left behind?"

"Not in Cassie. She's not like that." Cassie leaned toward him. "Let me tell you something

about my cousin. All her life, she wanted to be an artist, but when her mother got sick, she gave up all her dreams to take care of her. Does that sound like the type of person who'd deliberately hurt someone else?"

Jack's expression hardened. "Do-gooders are sometimes the ones you have to watch out for the most. All that pent-up rage and resentment has to boil over at some point."

Cassie's anger erupted before she could control it. "My cousin is not a do-gooder! She happens to be a decent human being who wouldn't hurt a flea. If you can't see that—"

"Hey, relax," he said softly. "I'm not attacking your cousin. I don't even know her."

"That's right, you don't." Cassie lifted her chin. "So let's just drop the subject. I really don't want to talk about her anymore."

"Nor do I," he agreed. "I'm not interested in this Cassie person because I happen to think you're right. I doubt she's behind any of this." His tone implied that she wouldn't have enough on the ball to plan such an elaborate scheme. "Let's just try to figure out who is."

Cassie nodded, but inside she seethed. A do-gooder? A *do-gooder?* How dare he? He didn't know anything about her. How dare he dismiss the years she'd spent lovingly tending her mother as the resentful actions of some…*do-gooder?*

"You didn't mention to anyone else that you'd be

at the beach house or on the boat, even in passing?" he pressed.

"No, but there is someone else who may have known about it," she admitted. "My roommate in L.A. Her name is Olivia D'Arby. She called the other night to tell me that she'd found my itinerary on the computer. That's how she located me at the Mirabelle. There may have been something about my trip to Galveston as well."

"*May* have been?"

"I don't really remember," Cassie said.

"Do you and this roommate get along?"

Cassie gave the question a moment of consideration. From their brief phone conversation, she'd gathered the relationship was strained at best. "I wouldn't say that. I think…well, she seems to think that she saw Owen Fleming first. I get the feeling she may resent…my relationship with him."

Cassie cringed. The last thing she wanted to talk about with Jack was Celeste's affair with Owen Fleming. She might resent his callous dismissal of her cousin—which was really her—as a do-gooder, but she still didn't want him to think of her as the kind of woman who was perfectly willing to involve herself with a married man in order to advance her career. But that's exactly what Celeste had done, wasn't it?

"Did you ever argue about him?"

Cassie had no idea, but she shook her head. "No, not really."

"What about the wife? According to the tabloids, she made some pretty ugly threats."

Cassie looked up in surprise. "You read the tabloids?"

Something flickered in his eyes. "I read a lot of things. Why?"

"It just seems strange, that's all." An Interpol agent who read the gossip columns? Didn't ring quite true, somehow.

"Is there any way Margo Fleming could have known you were in Galveston?"

"I don't see how...wait a minute." Cassie thought back to her conversation with the roommate. "Olivia said that someone had been by the apartment asking a lot of questions. She figured Margo had hired a private detective to dig up dirt on me. I suppose he could have followed me—" She gasped. "Oh, my God. I know who did it. Why didn't I think of it before? I know who blew up the boat!"

Jack looked skeptical. "Who?"

"The Gambinis."

He stared at her as if she'd taken leave of her senses. "The Gambinis. What are you talking about?"

Cassie's voice rose in excitement. "Someone told me recently that Margo Fleming is originally from Chicago, and that she has ties to the Gambini crime family. Blowing up a boat would be right up their alley, wouldn't it?"

"Just hold on a second before you get too carried

away. First of all, the Gambinis operate out of New York, and secondly, who told you that Margo Fleming has Mafia connections?"

Cassie shrugged. "Does it matter? If it's true, that could explain everything. The boat. The beach house. Everything."

"Yeah, except Mafia hit men don't usually miss their targets," Jack said dryly.

"No one's perfect. Besides, maybe they never meant to hurt me. Maybe they're just trying to warn me. As long as I stay away from Owen…" And that was a bit of a problem because Cassie would bet her last dollar that Celeste was even now off somewhere with Fleming. And she'd arranged for Cassie to remain behind to take the heat.

So tell him, a little voice urged Cassie. *Tell Jack the truth. He'll know what to do.*

And, of course, that would be the logical thing to do. Tell him the truth, and end the whole charade right then and there. Spill her guts, and *voilà.* The matter became Celeste's problem once again. Cassie could go back to her safe, nondescript little life and forget that any of this had ever happened.

Except for one thing.

She didn't want to.

Because in spite of the danger—or maybe even because of it—she'd never felt so energized. So *alive.* And she liked it. She liked being the center of attention. She liked having Jack Fury look at her…as if

he just might kiss her right then and there and be damned with the consequences.

Cassie had never had a man gaze at her in quite that way. Not a man like Jack, anyway. He was cool and hip and mysterious, and he moved through a world she could only imagine. A dark, dangerous, exciting world that Cassie wanted to be a part of, if even for a little while.

"Tell me about your relationship with Fleming," he said quietly.

Cassie glanced up. "I don't really like to talk about that."

Jack's gaze deepened. "I'm not judging you, Celeste."

"I know, it's just…I don't want you to think badly of me," she admitted.

Her candor seemed to surprise him. He reached out and took her hand, and that surprised Cassie. Then thrilled her. Even so innocent a contact made her have X-rated fantasies. Jack Fury seemed to bring out the worst in her. Or the best, depending on one's perspective.

He squeezed her fingers. "I'm hardly one to cast stones. I've done some things in my past I'm not exactly proud of, either."

"Really?" *Like what?* Cassie wanted to ask him.

"Sure." He shrugged. "I'm not perfect like that cousin you talked about. I've made mistakes just like everyone else."

Cassie sighed. Defending herself was getting old. "You've got the wrong idea about my cousin. She's far from perfect. She's made her share of mistakes, too. Take her wedding, for example. She had a change of heart at the last minute and practically left the groom standing at the altar."

Jack winced. "Now that's just cold."

Oh, you can forgive Celeste for having an affair with a married man, but you think I'm terrible for getting cold feet?

Cassie just couldn't win with this guy. He seemed determined to dislike her no matter how hard she tried to dissuade him of his preconceived notions—about her *and* Celeste. But she supposed she shouldn't be surprised that she couldn't compete with her glamorous cousin.

Still, she had one thing Celeste didn't have. She had Jack Fury's attention at the moment, and Cassie was suddenly determined to make the most it.

Who knows? Maybe by the time he finds out the truth, he'll be so in love with me that he won't care who I am.

Or who she wasn't.

But…was that really what she wanted? She'd just ended one relationship. Was she ready to jump into another?

Probably not. An involvement was the last thing she needed at the moment. Instead, Cassie knew she should be trying to get her head on straight, and then

decide what she wanted to do with the rest of her life. Romance would only complicate matters.

But a man like Jack Fury didn't come along every day, and Cassie wasn't ready to see the last of him. She had a sudden, burning desire to know everything there was to know about him. What he'd been like growing up. The kind of women he'd been involved with.

She would give a lot to have a few minutes alone with Betty Fury.

When Cassie glanced toward the bar, she found Jack's stepmother watching her. And she had a very strange look on her face, as if she recognized Cassie, but couldn't quite put her finger on where they'd met.

Cassie was getting that a lot lately. And it was funny because back home in Manville, no one had ever mistaken her for Celeste, possibly because her cousin had moved away years ago. Or possibly because the pretense had brought out a side of Cassie that she'd kept hidden for most of her adult life.

Maybe it wasn't so much the new clothes or the highlights in her hair that made her look like her cousin. Maybe it was her new attitude. Her new determination to live life to the fullest.

And Jack Fury seemed like a damn fine place to start to Cassie.

Chapter Nine

By the time they got back to the hotel, dusk had
fallen. Cassie expected Jack to drop her off, but instead, he pulled up in front of the Mirabelle and
handed his keys to the valet. As he came around the
car, Cassie studied him with surprise. "You don't
have to come in, you know. I'll be fine."

"Actually, I probably should have mentioned this
sooner, but I've booked a suite here. I'm in 3B."

Cassie's heart flip-flopped. "3B? But that's—"

"Right next door to you," he finished. "It's for
your own protection. I hope you don't mind."

Mind? Cassie was thrilled at the prospect of having him so near, but even as she conjured up all kinds
of interesting scenarios she tried to caution herself
about losing her head altogether. If Jack really was
on the trail of a jewel thief who had targeted Celeste's diamond, then keeping an eye on her suite made
sense.

But…and this was a very big but…

Cassie still didn't trust him. Not completely.

An Interpol agent on an undercover assignment in Houston, Texas? A jewel thief who had targeted Celeste out of all the rich, diamond-studded heiresses in the world? What were the chances?

And yet it was just far-fetched enough to be true. After all, maybe an international jewel thief would think he'd have easy pickings with the good old boys down in Houston. And Owen Fleming was certainly a big enough schmuck to broadcast his purchase of a ten-carat diamond ring for his mistress. Word could easily have gotten out about the three-million-dollar piece of jewelry. So yeah, Jack Fury's story could be true, and Cassie wanted to believe that it was.

But as they walked into the lobby, his father's warning rang in her ears. *"Watch out for that boy of mine. He's a real slick talker. Always has been."*

They were halfway across the lobby when she halted. "I don't have my room key. It was in my purse." Which was now at the bottom of the Gulf, probably in several hundred pieces. She shivered as the reality of her close call came back in full force.

"We'll get you another one from the front desk," Jack said.

The woman behind the registration counter looked up with a smile as they approached. "May I help you?"

"I've lost my key card," Cassie said. "I need to get another one."

"Of course, Miss Fortune." The clerk glanced at

her curiously, then began to type on the keyboard. She studied the computer screen for a moment. "I'm sorry, but I'll have to charge you for this one. It's hotel policy."

"No problem. Just put it on my account."

"And I'll need to see some form of identification."

"That's a bit of a problem," Cassie told her. "I lost my purse—"

Just then, Lyle Lester stepped out of his office and spotting Cassie, hurried over to the desk. "Is there a problem?" he asked anxiously. As usual, he was dressed all in black—black knit shirt, black jacket, slim black pants. His gaze went back and forth from Cassie to Jack, and something that might have been disapproval flickered across his brow.

"I've lost my purse," Cassie explained, "And unfortunately, I don't seem to be able to get a new key without my ID."

"I'll handle this," he said to the woman.

She glanced up in surprise, then shrugged. "Whatever you say, Mr. Lester."

She hurried off to busy herself at the other end of the counter while Lyle took over at the computer. Within moments he had programmed Cassie a new key card, which he produced with a slight bow. "Here you are. You're all set."

As Cassie took the key, her fingers brushed Lyle's, and a shiver went up her spine, but not the

good kind. She all but snatched the card from his hand. "Thank you."

His gaze moved to Jack. "I don't believe we've met."

"Jack Fury. I'm in 3B."

"Oh, yes, of course, Mr. Fury. You checked in yesterday, I believe. I trust your stay with us has been…satisfactory?"

Jack shrugged. "So far, so good."

"Excellent." Lyle shifted his focus back to Cassie. "And how was Galveston? We weren't expecting you back until tomorrow."

A warning shiver shot through Cassie. Jack was still standing behind her. She couldn't see his expression, but she could sense his keen interest. "How did you know I was in Galveston?" she tried to ask casually.

One brow lifted. "You asked us to make all the arrangements for you when you booked your suite. You don't remember?"

Cassie nodded. "Yes, of course. I'm sorry. It slipped my mind. And I suppose since you did make the arrangements that I should tell you the rental car is still in Galveston. Unfortunately, the car keys were also in my purse."

"Not to worry. I'll notify the rental agency immediately. If you could just give me the car's location…"

Cassie supplied the details, then she and Jack turned toward the elevator. He took her elbow—pos-

sessively she thought…hoped?—as they crossed the lobby.

"Somebody has a little crush," he said under his breath.

Color flooded Cassie's cheeks. Was she that transparent?

"Could he *be* any more obvious?" Jack muttered.

"Oh, you mean Lyle." *Whew.* "He says he's a fan."

"I'd say he's more than that. The guy was practically panting—"

Panting? *"Oh, my God."* Cassie whirled and grabbed Jack's arm. "We forgot Mr. Bogart! Sissy's going to kill me!"

"Sissy? Who's Sissy?"

"My cousin—" Cassie bit her lip. She was getting way too careless.

"The same cousin you talked about earlier? You called her Cassie before."

"Uh, Sissy was her nickname when we were little." *Nice save, Cass.*

Or maybe not. Jack's gaze narrowed in suspicion. "What does she have to do with Mr. Bogart?"

"She…she gave him to me. Yes, and she's still very protective of him. She'll kill me when she finds out what I've done."

"All right, calm down," Jack said. "I'll call my stepmother and ask her to take care of him until we can come pick him up. She's great with dogs. He's in good hands."

"Are you sure? Because Mr. Bogart can be a bit of a pill at times. And he doesn't exactly take to strangers." Except for Jack. The dog had warmed to him immediately, and Cassie wanted to assume that was a good sign. Unfortunately, she still couldn't get Stu Fury's warning out of her head. *Watch out for that boy of mine.*

"If Betty can handle my old man, I doubt Mr. Bogart will give her much trouble."

"You're probably right," Cassie murmured as the elevator doors opened.

They stepped inside, and as the doors slid closed, a feeling of déjà vu swept over Cassie. She couldn't help lifting her gaze to the ceiling. Had someone been on top of the elevator the other night?

"Is something wrong?" Jack asked.

She tried to shrug off her unease. "I guess everything is just now catching up with me. It's been quite a day."

"So tell me more about this cousin of yours."

Cassie turned in surprise. "Why? I thought you said you had no interest in her."

Jack shrugged. "Call it a hunch, but I'm starting to think she might somehow be involved in all this."

"She isn't." Not in the way he meant, anyway.

"How do you know? You said you hadn't been close in years. People change."

"Not…Cassie."

He gave her a strange look. "Once a do-gooder always a do-gooder?"

What was with the attitude? He'd never even met Cassie. Well, at least, he didn't know that he had. Why had he taken such an apparent disliking to her?

And what was it about Celeste that made a man like Jack Fury lose his perspective so utterly? That made him willing—almost eager—to overlook *her* flaws?

Would he ever be able to look at Cassie the way he looked at the woman he thought was Celeste?

No, because you're not his type. You're not exciting. You aren't the least bit glamorous. Face it, you're just a poor imitation of your cousin, and when Jack finds out how you've tricked him—

Okay, so she'd just have to make sure he didn't find out. Because once he knew the truth, she might never see him again. Not without a sheet of bulletproof glass between them, anyway.

For now, she would do just what she'd promised herself to do. She'd live for the moment. She'd have herself a little adventure and let the future sort itself out.

Because this was the new Cassie, after all. No, this was the *real* Cassie. A woman determined to embrace life at any cost.

Right now, though, she'd rather embrace Jack Fury.

Because trustworthy or not, the man was seriously sexy.

As if reading her mind again, he lifted a hand to

her cheek, and every nerve ending in Cassie's body tingled. She felt as if she'd been plugged into a giant electrical outlet.

"You have sand on your face," he murmured.

She gulped. "I do?"

His gaze deepened as his fingers brushed across her skin, and for one brief moment, Cassie could have sworn he was going to kiss her. His touch lingered and...the elevator pinged.

He didn't even notice. He couldn't seem to tear his gaze from hers.

His head lowered. He *was* going to kiss her. Cassie held her breath.

And then the doors slid open.

"Well, hello," a surprised voice said from the hallway. "Are you two getting off?"

If Cassie had her way....

She glanced toward the door, and seeing Mrs. Ambrose-Pritchard's curious expression, she took a step away from Jack. "Oh, hello, Mrs. Ambrose...Pritchard..."

"It's Evelyn, remember?" She trained her blue gaze on Jack, who had his thumb pressed against the open button. "And who is this?"

"This is Jack Fury," Cassie supplied quickly. "Mrs. Ambrose-Pritchard."

"It's a pleasure," Jack murmured.

"Oh, the pleasure is all mine." She presented him a delicate hand as she stepped onto the elevator.

Jack took her arched fingers and hesitated for a moment, as if not quite knowing what to do with them. Then he gave her hand a gentle shake before exiting the elevator behind Cassie.

"Celeste, dear, did you have a good time in Galveston?"

Cassie whirled. "How did you—"

The doors slid closed, hiding Mrs. Ambrose-Pritchard's expression.

"You told her you were going to Galveston?" Jack asked.

"No, I never said a word. How in the world could she have known?"

"I don't know," he said with a pensive frown. "But it seems our suspect list just got a little longer."

As THEY WALKED toward Celeste's suite, Jack could hear the phone ringing inside, but instead of hurrying to unlock the door, she merely leaned against the wall and stared up at him. Her makeup had long since worn away, and the freckles he'd glimpsed earlier were now even more pronounced. They spilled across the bridge of her nose and onto her cheekbones, making her seem young and vulnerable and utterly alluring.

Those freckles added an interesting dimension to her features, Jack decided, because they were such a contrast to the rest of her. There was nothing innocent or vulnerable about that body of hers. It was curvy and soft and all woman.

He had the strongest urge to finish what he'd started in the elevator, but the interruption had probably been for the best. Getting involved with a woman like her was not the smartest move a guy like him could make. He was just a working-class stiff, and she was…*way out of your league, Jackie.*

Yeah, yeah, he knew all that. Unfortunately, certain parts of his anatomy hadn't received the message yet.

She was still staring up at him through her lashes. They were dark except for the tips, which were golden. Funny how all of a sudden he was noticing all sorts of enticing little details about her.

"Would you like to come in for a nightcap?" she asked almost shyly.

"A nightcap? We haven't even had dinner yet. As a matter of fact…" The telephone kept right on ringing, and Jack glanced at the door. "Don't you want to get that?"

"In a minute." But she still made no move to open the door, and Jack decided she must be avoiding someone's call.

When the ringing finally stopped, he saw her let out a long breath. Only then did she unlock the door. "You were saying something about dinner?"

He cleared his throat. "Yes, I was just about to ask you—"

No sooner had she opened the door, than the phone started to ring again.

"Maybe you should get that," he muttered.

She glanced reluctantly inside the suite. "They'll call back."

Who was she trying to evade? Jack wondered. Owen Fleming?

He wanted to believe that, he realized. He wanted to believe that she'd really meant it when she said her involvement with Fleming was over. And Jack didn't want to hold the indiscretion against her because, frankly, he hadn't exactly been Mr. Innocent himself.

Still, in spite of his attraction to her—and he was attracted to her, no denying that—he couldn't help feeling a little disappointed that a woman who seemed so perfect in every other way could let herself be used by a creep like Fleming.

And what makes you any better? his conscience demanded. Wasn't he using her, too?

It was a question he didn't want to dwell on.

"Could be important," he said. "I don't think they're going to give up until you answer."

"Oh, all right." She walked across the room and snatched up the phone. "Hello? Hello?" Just as quickly, she hung it back up and glanced at him. "Must have been a wrong number." But Jack thought he detected a flicker of fear in her eyes.

He stepped into the room and closed the door behind him. "What's going on?"

"What do you mean?"

"That phone call shook you up," he said. "You want to tell me why?"

"It's just…" She hesitated. "I've been getting some hang ups lately. It's a little unnerving after what happened the other night."

He moved closer. "What are you talking about?"

She lifted her shoulders dismissively, but a trace of fear still glimmered in her eyes. "I received…a threatening phone call."

Jack tensed. "Threatening how?"

"Nothing really overt. It was probably nothing—"

"When was this?"

"Right after I saw you at Metro the other night." She seemed reluctant to talk about it. Or maybe she just didn't want him to see how scared she really was.

She sighed. "Look, it was probably nothing…just someone's idea of a prank. I wouldn't even have given it much thought except…well…" She glanced away. "Something else happened. Besides the incident at the restaurant, I mean."

Jack frowned. "Maybe you'd better start at the beginning and tell me everything."

She nodded. "Yes, I think I should. Like I said, it was probably nothing, but with everything that happened today…" She wrapped her arms around her middle. "After I left Metro that night, I came back to the hotel, and as I was heading up here to my room, the power went off. I got stuck in the elevator for a few minutes, and I heard this noise…like maybe

someone was on top of the elevator and they were…I don't know…going to come down through that little door in the ceiling and…whatever…" She trailed away on a shudder. "Anyway, the electricity was only off for a few minutes, and afterward I came straight up to my suite. That's when I got the phone call."

"What did the caller say?"

"'Did I scare you?' I had the impression he was referring to the elevator incident."

Jack's frowned deepened. "Did you recognize the voice?"

She shook her head.

"But you know that it was a man?"

"No, not really. Whoever it was used one of those electronic gadgets to disguise his voice. Or her voice. When I asked who it was, the caller said 'Open the door and find out.' And then someone knocked on my door."

"What did you do?"

She lifted her chin. "Well, I didn't open the door if that's what you're thinking. I've got more sense than that. But I did go over and look out the peephole. I didn't see anyone at first, but then someone knocked again a minute or two later. When I looked out that time, I saw Lyle Lester."

Jack's gaze sharpened. "Lester? What'd he want?"

"He said that the night clerk had seen me get on the elevator right before the electricity went off, and he wanted to make sure I was okay. And I guess that

makes sense except...I don't understand how the night clerk could have seen me. She wasn't at the front desk when I came in. No one was."

"So what do you think happened?"

"I don't know. The thought has crossed my mind that maybe Lyle is the one who saw me. Maybe he turned the power off to scare me, then followed me up here and made that call on a cell phone from the hallway. I know it sounds crazy." She bit her lip. "But there's just something about him that gives me the creeps. I noticed it when I first saw him in the alley the other night."

"What night was that?"

"The night that poor woman was murdered in Montrose."

Lyle Lester had been in the alley? On the night of the murder? They were entering dangerous territory here. Jack had also been in the alley that night. And he'd come face-to-face with Celeste.

The conversation had suddenly gotten very dicey because Jack needed to find out about Lyle Lester without having Celeste recall certain other details about that night.

"Are you sure it was the same night?"

She nodded. "Oh, yes. I remember it distinctly because I couldn't get what happened to that poor woman off my mind. And I kept hearing all those sirens. That's why I went out to the balcony. I was already on edge, and then I saw a strange man standing

in the alley staring up at me. I thought at first he might be the murderer. I even imagined…don't laugh…I even thought for a minute he could be Casanova."

Jack wasn't laughing. "Why did you think that?"

"I'd just heard a criminal psychologist on television talk about those murders last summer. And she mentioned a police detective she'd worked with who still believes Casanova is out there somewhere."

Jack's heart skipped a beat. "What police detective?"

She shrugged. "Someone who worked on the case. Anyway, when I saw a man in the alley, I let my imagination run away with me. But then Lyle told me later that I'd seen him."

Jack relaxed a little. "What was he doing out there?"

"He said some of the kitchen staff had seen a homeless person going through the Dumpsters, and he'd gone outside to check it out for himself. And I suppose that's entirely possible because earlier I'd seen someone out there, too. The creep even kicked poor Mr. Bogart."

"*Kicked* him?" Jack blurted in outrage. "I did no such thing!"

Chapter Ten

Cassie stared at him in confusion. "What?"

"What?" Jack repeated.

"I said some creep kicked Mr. Bogart and you said 'I did no such thing.' What did you mean by that?" she demanded.

"You must have misunderstood me. What I said was, 'Who would do such a thing?' Who would kick a poor, defenseless little dog like Mr. Bogart?"

Cassie said doubtfully, "But that's not what you said—"

"I can tell you one thing," Jack cut in. "If I ever get my hands on that sorry SOB, he'll think twice before he kicks another animal."

The conviction in his voice stunned Cassie. "Wow," she said in awe. "You really feel passionate about that, don't you?" He certainly seemed to have a special affinity for animals. Cassie thought again about the way Mr. Bogart had reacted to him, and she decided that had to say something about the man's character.

"I just don't like seeing anyone or anything mistreated." His blue gaze met hers. "I guess it brings out my protective instincts."

This side of Jack Fury was definitely bringing out something in Cassie. When he looked at her that way, she wanted to fling caution—and her clothes—to the wind.

She imagined the two of them naked and entwined on her bed, Jack all protective and her all submissive.

"Go on."

Cassie tried to clear her brain. "I figured the guy I saw was just some weirdo or pervert or something, but Lyle said he was probably Old Joe."

"Who's Old Joe?"

"A homeless guy who goes through the Dumpsters now and then. Supposedly, he's harmless, but after what he did to Mr. Bogart and then to Mrs. Ambrose-Pritchard, I'm not so sure."

Jack shook his head. "Now I'm really confused. How does Mrs. Ambrose-Pritchard figure into this?"

"She was attacked in the alley later that same night."

Jack's brows shot up. "*Attacked?* By this Old Joe person?"

"We don't know for sure. She didn't get a good look at him, but whoever it was shoved her down and hurt her ankle so badly that Lyle had to carry her back to her suite."

"Lester was the one who found her?"

"No, I did when I took Mr. Bogart out for another walk. Lyle was just sort of there lurking in the shadows. He nearly scared us half to death."

"What reason did he give for being in the alley that time?"

"Still looking for Old Joe, I guess." She paused, her brow furrowed in thought. "Another interesting thing about that whole night was Mrs. Ambrose-Pritchard's reaction to Lyle. She seems to detest him."

"Any idea why?"

"No, and I didn't ask. After she told me about Margo Fleming's connection to the Gambinis, I just wanted to come back here and—"

"Wait a minute. Mrs. Ambrose-Pritchard is the one who told you about the Gambinis?"

"Yes. Why?"

Jack ran a hand through his blond hair. "I don't know. There's just something about all this that sounds a little fishy to me."

"Fishy, how?"

"You say Mrs. Ambrose-Pritchard hurt her ankle so badly she couldn't walk back to her room. An injury like that can take days or even weeks to heal. But I didn't notice a limp earlier when she got on the elevator."

Come to think of it, Cassie hadn't, either. "But…why would she pretend to be hurt if she wasn't?"

"A lawsuit, maybe?" Jack shrugged. "Who knows? I'd say one thing is certain, though. Someone is trying to do a real number on you. Maybe all they want is to frighten you, but it's clear to me that you're the target of someone's animosity."

"The jewel thief?" Cassie suggested. "Maybe he's behind all this—"

"Forget about the jewel thief," Jack said flatly.

"Why?"

"The phone call, the boat, the trashed beach house. That's not the work of a professional. That's personal."

Cassie shivered at his tone, at the dark glimmer in his eyes, and then, as if on cue, the phone rang again, startling her. Her gaze darted to the phone, then back to Jack. "Should I get that?"

He nodded, then quickly followed her to the phone. When he'd positioned himself beside her, he motioned for her to pick it up. As Cassie lifted the receiver, he put his ear next to hers so that he could listen in. His proximity caused Cassie's pulse to leap.

"Hello?" she breathed.

"Miss Fortune? This is Sergeant Vargas. I'm sorry to disturb you, but I've been trying to track down Jack. He's not answering his cell phone. Do you happen to know where I can reach him?"

"He's right here, Sergeant," she said in relief. She handed the receiver to Jack. As he lifted it to his ear, she backed away. The moment their physical contact

ended, she could breathe again. Funny how that worked.

"What have you got?" Jack listened for a moment, then scribbled something on a notepad. "No, never heard of it. Well, that's interesting…"

He talked for several more minutes, and by the time he finally hung up, Cassie was on pins and needles. "What did he say?"

"The Jaguar is registered to a company here in Houston called the Sheridan Group. It's a research and development outfit founded by the family of Ethan Gold's late wife, Alaina."

Gold's late wife? Cassie hadn't even known he'd been married. That was another tidbit her cousin had neglected to tell her. But to be fair, perhaps Celeste hadn't known that Cassie would get caught up in all this intrigue.

Then again, maybe she had…

"At the time of his wife's death, Gold inherited his wife's stock and a seat on the board of directors, along with substantial properties here in Houston, the beach house in Galveston, a cabin in Colorado, and a condo in Hawaii." Jack gave Cassie a look she couldn't quite define before walking over to the window to glance out. "The really interesting part of all this is that Alaina Gold died seven years ago. She was shot during a home invasion. No one was ever arrested for her murder."

"My God," Cassie whispered.

Jack turned back to face her, his expression grim. "Vargas tracked down the detective who headed up the investigation. He's retired now, but he remembered the case very well. He said that Gold was at the top of their suspect list, but they didn't have enough evidence to make an arrest."

Cassie's heart beat so hard she felt breathless. She knew Jack was leading up to something, but she didn't know what.

He studied her for a moment. "You were still in Houston seven years ago, weren't you? You and Gold were close back then. You even lived together for a while. Was that before or after his wife died?"

Cassie gasped. He couldn't think— "You're not suggesting that my...that I had something to do with his wife's death, are you?"

Jack shrugged. "I'm not suggesting anything. But at the very least, Gold's past casts a suspicious light on his character. And it gives us reason to believe he may have a violent history."

"You think Ethan is the one responsible for blowing up his own boat?" Cassie asked incredulously. "For ransacking his own beach house? Why would he do that?"

Jack shrugged again. "Maybe he thinks you know something about his wife's death. Maybe he's afraid you'll somehow implicate him."

"After seven years?"

"I'm only guessing, of course. When you talked

to him last, did he give you any indication that he might be getting paranoid?"

"Not…that I recall." It was Cassie who turned away this time to wrestle with her own conscience. Now was the time to come clean with Jack. To tell him she couldn't answer his questions because she wasn't Celeste. Now was the time to make sure that she covered her own butt in all this.

So…why didn't she? Why didn't she tell Jack the truth and let him walk out that door? "If he really wanted to kill me, why would he use his own boat?" she wondered aloud. "He'd have to know that would make him a prime suspect. Again. Why would he take such a chance?"

"That's a good question." Jack started across the room toward the door. "Let's go see if he has a good answer."

"Right now?" Cassie asked in alarm.

"No time like the present." Pausing at the door, Jack glanced back. "Are you coming?"

He didn't have to ask her twice.

IN SPITE OF THE yuppie invasion of the eighties, West University remained a charming and sophisticated enclave with its tree-lined streets and Cape Cod Revival-style architecture. The neighborhood's proximity to the Museum District, the Medical Center and Rice University made it one of the most desirable locations in the city, which was why many of

the original homes had been torn down in the past twenty years to make room for modern-day replicas. But the new blended so seamlessly with the old that the impact on the area was barely perceptible.

As they drove along the quaint streets, Cassie tried to appreciate the neighborhood's beauty, but her mind kept racing. Who was out to get Celeste? Or at the very least, who wanted to scare the living daylights out of her? And more important, what was her cousin's part in all this? Had she deliberately set Cassie up?

She didn't want to believe her cousin capable of such a betrayal, but they hadn't been close in years. She had no idea how much Celeste might have changed, and self-preservation could be a powerful motivation.

Cassie now found herself caught between the proverbial rock and a hard place. If she told Jack the truth, their relationship would be over before it had even started, and worse, she might even face jail time.

She had no idea if she'd done anything illegal. She'd used Celeste's name and her credit card, not to mention taking Ethan Gold's boat out under false pretenses. For all Cassie knew, she could be held liable for the damages. She could even be charged with fraud and God only knew what other crimes. If the police arrested her she might have to remain behind bars for days or even weeks before her cousin finally came forward to clear her.

What if she didn't come forward? Cassie thought suddenly. If Celeste knew her life was in danger, she might let Cassie linger in jail indefinitely.

On the other hand, if Cassie didn't come clean soon, *she* could end up dead.

Between the two options, those orange jumpsuits were looking better and better.

Still, there just might be another way out if she could buy herself some time. Celeste couldn't stay in hiding forever. She'd have to surface sooner or later.

"This is it." Jack slowed the car.

Cassie stared at the darkened house as they drove past. "Doesn't look like anyone's home."

"Or maybe that's what he wants people to think." Jack drove to the end of the block and pulled to the curb. Turning off the ignition, he reached for the door handle.

"What are you doing?" Cassie asked in alarm.

"I figured I'd have a look around."

Her gaze widened. "You're not going to break into his house, are you?"

"No, of course not. But there're other ways of finding information."

"Like going through his trash?"

Jack's head whipped around. "What do you mean?"

Cassie shrugged. "I saw it in a movie once. A cop found evidence to put away a killer by going through

his trash. Yikes. I'd hate to think of someone doing that to me, but then, I'm not a killer. And I suppose in police work the end justifies the means, doesn't it?"

Jack stared at her for a moment longer, then glanced away. "Sometimes." He got out of the car. "Lock the doors behind me. I won't be long."

Cassie pushed the lock button as she hunkered down in the seat and watched him in the rearview mirror until he disappeared from her sight. Then she glanced nervously around the neighborhood, hoping that no one would spot the car and call the police. She wasn't in the mood for lengthy explanations, and she wasn't sure the cops would buy what she had to tell them even with Jack's corroboration.

"Well, Cassie," she muttered. "This is another fine mess you've gotten us into."

To think, back in Manville her biggest concern was being hexed by Minnie Cantrell. Cassie shivered. Considering everything that had happened in the past couple of days, maybe the old bat had some supernatural powers, after all.

THE HOUSE had appeared completely dark from the street, but as Jack approached from the opposite direction, he could see a light in the rear.

Slipping behind a neatly trimmed hedge, he reconnoitered the street for a moment before making his move. It was still relatively early, and he was

surprised by how quiet the neighborhood was. Only an occasional car drove by.

Plastering himself against the side of the house, he inched toward the lighted window that he'd spotted from the street. As he drew alongside it, a dog began to bark from somewhere nearby, and he froze. A silhouette appeared in the window for one brief moment, but from his position, he couldn't make out who it was.

He waited for several minutes after the shadow disappeared before easing up to the glass. Glancing through, he saw nothing at first, and then his heart bucked wildly as a woman came into view. She had on dark glasses and what he thought was a wig, but he recognized her, anyway.

She walked quickly to the door, then paused to say something over her shoulder to someone Jack couldn't see.

A split second later, a well-groomed Chihuahua trotted over and followed her out the door.

WHEN JACK RAPPED on the driver's window a few minutes later, Cassie let out a breath of relief as she disengaged the lock.

"That didn't take long," she said as he slid behind the wheel. "Did you find anything—" She broke off on a gasp as she realized that the man climbing into the car wasn't Jack at all, but someone she'd never seen before.

Terrified, she made a grab for the door handle, but the man's hand shot out and stopped her. His other hand came over her mouth as she tried to scream.

"I'm not going to hurt you. I just want to talk to you, okay?"

When she continued to struggle, he said, "I'll remove my hand, but if you scream, I'll be forced to do something drastic. I might even call the police and tell them who you really are. You don't want that, do you?"

Cassie went dead still.

"That's better." He removed his hand from her mouth, but the other one held fast to her wrist.

"Who are you?" Cassie breathed.

"I would ask you the same thing, but I already know the answer. You're the cousin." He released her then and draped one arm over the back of her seat, staring at her intently in the dark. "Cassie, isn't it?"

Her heart thudded even harder. "Who are you?" she asked again. "How do you know me?"

"Come on. You must have some idea."

"Professor Gold?"

He smiled.

The hair at the back of Cassie's neck rose at that smile. She remembered, suddenly, everything Jack had told her earlier about Gold. *"The really interesting part of all this is that Alaina Gold died seven years ago. She was shot during a home invasion. No one was ever arrested for her murder."*

Cassie gulped. "What do you want?"

He shrugged and moved in closer. So close Cassie could have sworn she saw a diabolical twinkle in his dark eyes. "All I want from you is a little cooperation."

She pressed herself against the door to get away from him.

He laughed when he saw what she was doing. "Relax. I'm not going to hurt you. Assuming we're able to strike a bargain, of course."

The door handle dug into Cassie's ribs. "What kind of bargain?"

He was so close now she could feel his warm breath on her face. He smelled faintly of peppermint, which seemed like an oddly comforting scent for a man like him. "You get your friend to stop snooping in my business, and I won't go to the police."

Cassie crossed her arms and inched her fingers toward the door handle. "What makes you think I have anything to hide from the police?"

"You're running around town masquerading as Celeste, staying in an exclusive hotel, eating at expensive restaurants, going on shopping sprees. Not to mention stealing my boat. Last time I heard, that's a felony. You could be looking at some serious jail time."

Cassie's fingers curled around the handle. "But Celeste knows what I'm doing. It was her idea."

"And she'd come forward to clear you?"

"Of course."

"How do you know?"

"Because—"

"Do you know where she is?"

"No, but—"

"How to reach her?"

Cassie hesitated. "No."

"Then at the very least, you could spend a few unpleasant days in jail with some very unpleasant people until your cousin decides to surface and clear you. If she does."

Cassie had already thought of all that herself, but she tried to assume a confident air. "Of course, she'll clear me. Why wouldn't she?"

Gold shrugged. "Celeste can be a bit capricious at times. No one knows that better than I. What if she went off to Europe to lick her wounds and forgot all about you? You'd be left holding the bag, wouldn't you?"

Cassie's confidence quickly deflated. She hadn't considered the possibility that her cousin might have left the country. "Okay, you've made your point," she conceded. "We both know why I don't want to involve the cops, but what about you? What are you so afraid of?"

Too late, Cassie realized her mistake. Pushing Ethan Gold into a corner was not a good idea.

"Let's just say, the cops could make my life un-

pleasant, as well," he said softly. "Do we have a deal?"

Cassie had a feeling she was making a deal with the devil, but she wanted him gone so she nodded.

He opened the car door, then turned to stare at her in the sudden glare. "You don't really look that much like Celeste, you know. I'm surprised you've been able to pull this off for as long as you have."

Then he climbed out of the car, closed the door with hardly a sound, and was gone before Cassie had time to catch her breath.

SOMEONE TAPPED on the car window, and the faint sound startled Cassie so badly she banged her head against the glass. She spun, her heart in her throat, but this time, it was Jack who stared down at her. She released the locks, and he went around to the driver's side to climb in.

Cassie had never been so glad to see anyone in her life. She felt tempted to throw her arms around his neck and hang on tight, but then, in the brief second before he closed the door and doused the light, she saw a trickle of blood at his temple. "Oh, my God, Jack. You're bleeding! Are you all right?"

"I've been better." He leaned forward and started the engine.

"What happened?" Cassie asked worriedly.

He shrugged. "Ran into a hedge. Guess I'm getting sloppy."

She could have wept in relief. For a moment there she'd been afraid he might have run into Ethan Gold. "Did you…see anything?"

"Like what?"

His tone puzzled her. He sounded almost…angry. *Oh, no.* He *had* seen Ethan Gold. Maybe he'd even spotted him getting out of the car. Did he think now that Cassie—Celeste—was somehow involved with Gold? Did he think they'd conspired to kill Gold's wife seven years ago?

"Jack, there's something I need to tell you."

"What is it?" He turned then and the look in his eyes made her falter.

Cassie bit her lip. What if she told Jack the truth and he didn't believe her? What if he turned her in?

And maybe that had been Celeste's intent all along. Maybe she'd committed a crime and planned for Cassie to take the fall.

Even if she somehow managed to convince Jack of the truth, he might not be so willing to help her once he learned who she was. He might just turn her over to the cops and wash his hands of the whole affair.

Okay, so she couldn't just blurt everything out to him. She had to find the right time and the right way to tell him so that her confession didn't end up coming back to bite her on the butt.

"You had something you wanted to tell me?" Jack pressed.

Cassie glanced away from that penetrating gaze. "Are you…sure you're okay? That scratch looks pretty deep."

"I'm fine." If possible, his expression grew even darker as he put the car in gear and pulled away from the curb.

Cassie didn't understand what had happened, but his new attitude worried her. What had he seen? What did he know? And, most important, could she trust him?

She really, really, *really* needed to talk to Celeste. In hindsight, Cassie realized she should have insisted on having a number where her cousin could be reached. In hindsight, she realized a lot of things.

She said tentatively, "Where are we going?"

He scowled at the road. "Back to the hotel to regroup. Unless you have a better idea."

"No, that's fine."

A few minutes later, they arrived at the Mirabelle and rode the elevator in silence to the third floor. Once again, Jack walked her to her suite, but this time he didn't linger. Nor did he mention dinner.

Instead he said wearily, "It's been a long day. We both need to get some rest. We'll get together tomorrow and try to figure out where to go from here."

Cassie nodded in disappointment, but at least he'd lost the attitude. Whatever had been bothering him in the car seemed to have faded now that they were back at the hotel. He was almost like the old Jack again, Cassie thought. Almost, but not quite.

"You know where to reach me," he said. "And you have my cell phone number, right? If anything happens, anything at all, you call me."

She nodded again.

When he turned away, she said very softly, "Jack?"

He glanced over his shoulder. "Yeah?"

"Are you sure you're okay? You're still bleeding."

He touched a fingertip to the scratch. "I'm fine. Don't worry about me…Celeste."

Was it her imagination or had he hesitated over her cousin's name?

Once again he started for his suite and once again Cassie called him back. "Jack?"

"Yeah?"

"I never got around to thanking you. I'm grateful for everything you did today."

He shrugged. "No problem. That's what I'm trained to do."

She nodded.

He turned.

"Jack?"

This time, instead of answering her, he spun and putting his hands on her arms, he backed her up against the wall. His mouth came down on hers so fast and so furiously, Cassie didn't have time to even gasp. The assault left her stunned. She couldn't think, couldn't respond. For a moment, all she could do was cling to him helplessly.

Then her body took over and she opened her mouth beneath his. Her tongue met his, desperate thrust for desperate thrust, as her arms wrapped tightly around him and she pressed herself against him.

He groaned into her mouth.

She groaned into his.

And all the while he kept right on kissing her. Kissing her so deeply that Cassie felt herself coming apart at the seams.

When he finally pulled away, she leaned her head weakly against the wall. *Oh...my...God...*

"That was...wow." She fanned herself. "I don't think I've ever been kissed like that in my life."

The old Jack grinned down at her. "I guess you inspired me."

"I guess," she said in awe. And who would have thought it? Because that was *her,* Cassie Boudreaux, who had been kissing him and not Celeste.

And, man oh man, did she, Cassie Boudreaux, ever want to kiss him again. His mouth was just begging her to.

She stared up at him, drinking in every detail of his face. Those baby-blue eyes that had deepened with passion. The high cheekbones, the straight nose and strong jaw...he was one *fine*-looking man, no question.

And looking finer by the minute.

And that body, all lean and sexy and hard in all the right places.

"Do you…" She moistened her lips "…want to come inside?"

He slid his mouth along her throat, then nuzzled her ear. "You know I do."

"Well, then…"

He cupped her neck beneath her hair. "I can't think of anything I'd rather do than…come inside."

Cassie just about lost it then. His voice was like a velvety purr…and that mouth. Oh, God, that mouth was not even an inch from her own. "Well, then…"

He kissed her again, quick and hard, and then he stared down at her for a moment, his expression enigmatic. "I don't think it would be such a good idea."

"Why not?" Because it sounded like a spectacular idea to Cassie.

"We've both been operating on an adrenaline high for hours. I think we need to come back down to earth and let you think things through before you do something you might regret in the morning."

But she wouldn't regret it. Cassie just knew it.

She cleared her throat. "You don't have to play the hero. I'm a big girl. And this is the twenty-first century, remember?" Consenting adults could have sex without regrets. They did it all the time.

Jack drew a finger along her jawline. "You don't know what you're letting yourself in for. There's a lot about me you don't know."

"There's a lot about me *you* don't know."

"Like what?" His voice hardened almost imperceptibly. "What is it I don't know about you?" He trailed his finger down her throat.

Cassie shivered at his touch. "A girl can't give away all her secrets, now can she?" She wrapped her hand around his finger and drew it to her mouth, teasing the tip with her tongue.

Something like a shudder went through his whole body, and he closed his eyes for a moment as if trying to collect himself. When he looked at her again, his eyes were like laser beams burning into hers. "You're a very dangerous woman."

His words thrilled Cassie. Her? A dangerous woman? *Cool.*

Chapter Eleven

The moment Cassie closed the door, she spun to peer out the peephole. Jack was still out there. Even after she turned the dead bolt and fastened the safety lock, he lingered just outside her door. She even saw him lift his hand once as if to knock, and then, thinking better of it, he turned away.

Only then did Cassie tear herself away from the peephole and collapse weakly against the door.

Her heart started to thud again as she closed her eyes and recalled every detail of Jack's kisses. The way his lips had felt against hers, the way his body had pressed into hers...

Cassie had never had a kiss effect her so powerfully, and she told herself that her pounding heart and trembling legs were the result of a very potent physical attraction and nothing more. She'd wanted Jack Fury from the moment she'd laid eyes on him.

But even though all that was true, Cassie had a

sneaking suspicion more was at play here. If she wasn't careful, she just might fall in love with him.

Would that be so terrible? Her engagement to Danny Cantrell hadn't worked out, but that didn't mean Cassie was incapable of sustaining a relationship, did it? Danny just hadn't been the right man for her. He was content with his life in Manville. He was a big fish in a little pond, and Cassie couldn't imagine him living anywhere else any more than she could imagine herself going back there, even when all this ended.

And it would end. Celeste would come back and reclaim her life, and Cassie would have to find one of her own. What that life would be like, she had no idea, but she was ready for it. Eager for it. And if Jack Fury was a part of it, so much the better.

But he wouldn't be, would he? He was a part of Celeste's life. When he found out who Cassie really was, he'd have no need to stick around any longer. He'd move on and so would she. Eventually.

Cassie sighed as she tried to push away all those annoying thoughts and just concentrate on Jack's kisses. Because the man could kiss. Seriously. And if he could kiss like that, she could only imagine—

Her eyes popped open as something dark and scary slithered into her thoughts.

There was no sound in the room, no movement on the balcony, nothing that should have scared her, but suddenly Cassie was frightened.

A chill crept up her backbone as her frantic gaze searched the room. Nothing seemed amiss or out of place. The cushions on the sofa were perfectly straight. The lamp she'd left on earlier glowed from the corner desk. The French doors across the room were closed and secured.

And yet…something was different.

Cassie couldn't put her finger on what it was, but she knew that someone had been in her room while she'd been out.

Her first instinct was to run screaming into the hallway, but she forced back her panic as she took a step inside the room. The bedroom door was open, and a light was on. From her position, Cassie could see the bed. The covers were neatly turned down, and there were mints on the pillow.

She put a hand to her heart, trying to calm herself. Okay, mystery solved. The maid had been in while she was out. No cause for alarm. No reason to call Jack and have him rush right over, although that had been Cassie's second instinct.

But if she called him so quickly after he'd just left her, he might think it was a ploy on her part to get him into her room. And into her bed. Cassie couldn't honestly deny that a part of her was looking for any excuse to do just that.

So she wouldn't call him. She did have some measure of pride, she supposed. But…the room seemed so quiet. And empty.

Cassie couldn't help feeling unnerved by the silence, and then she suddenly realized why she felt so uneasy. So alone. She missed Mr. Bogart. In spite of her dispassion for dogs, she'd become attached to the little guy, and now his was another presence in her life that she'd have to give up when Celeste returned.

If she returned…

Of course, she'd come back. Once the publicity surrounding her affair with Owen Fleming died down, she'd be ready to retake Hollywood by storm.

Cassie put a hand to her mouth. Was that it? Was Celeste's comeback the catalyst behind everything that had happened to Cassie?

What if her cousin had staged the whole charade—exploding boat and all—in order to win back the public's sympathy? What if Cassie was just a pawn? A gullible, expendable pawn.

Another thought suddenly occurred to her. What if Jack was in on it? What if he'd been playing Cassie, too? Wouldn't that explain how he'd just happened to be so Johnny-on-the-spot at the restaurant and then when the boat had exploded? And now here at the hotel? He and Celeste could be working together to set her up, but for what?

Cassie had a terrible feeling she was on to something. Celeste was playing her, and she obviously had an accomplice. Cassie didn't want to believe it was Jack, but his complicity made a certain amount of sense.

But there was also the roommate, Olivia D'Arby. And Ethan Gold. Yes, Gold as an accomplice made even more sense than Jack. He and Celeste had a history, and if they'd been responsible for Alaina Gold's murder, then…what else might they be capable of?

Cassie went into the bathroom to get ready for bed, and for a few minutes, her nightly routine took her mind off her problems.

But by the time she crawled under the covers, her mind was racing again with all the disturbing possibilities. Folding her arms behind her head, she stared at the ceiling, knowing she wouldn't be able to get a wink of sleep that night.

SHE WAS sleeping like a baby.

Celeste didn't know if that was a testament to her cousin's clean conscience or her own stealth, but whatever the reason, Cassie didn't move a muscle as Celeste approached the bed.

Amazing how similar their facial features were when their personalities could not be more different. Not to mention their bodies, although Celeste supposed there were some men left in the world who preferred a more curvaceous figure. But those men weren't among the movers and shakers in Hollywood so Celeste had had to learn early on how to play the game.

Poor Cassie. She had no idea what a dog-eat-dog world it was out there. But she was about to find out. The hard way.

Chapter Twelve

"Surprise!" Cher laughed at the look on Jack's face the next morning when he answered her knock. He was shirtless, and his hair was all messy, as if he'd just gotten out of bed. He was also sporting a night's growth of beard, which she found pretty damn sexy.

Too bad the guy was a real nutcase when it came to his work, Cher thought as her gaze slipped over him. She supposed his intensity had something to do with his mother's murder.

Jack didn't know she knew about that, of course. He never talked about it, but one night the two of them had had one too many margaritas, and to Cher's surprise, he'd finally opened up to her.

His mother had been killed when the family restaurant had been held up one night. It was after hours, and she'd been closing up alone when two gunmen had come in and shot her dead for the sixty-seven bucks they'd found in the cash register.

Jack and one of his brothers had found her an

hour later, lying in a pool of blood. He'd never gotten over it, he'd confided to Cher. He still dreamed about it. Seeing his mother like that was what had made him decide to become a cop and why he was so determined to bring every criminal to justice. Because his mother's killers had never been found.

That hidden intensity and his slightly neurotic personality would make him impossible to live with, Cher thought. But his quirkiness was also what made him damn attractive.

He scratched his arm. "What are you doing here?"

"Is that any way to greet your personal shopper?" She held up a plastic bag. "I've been hitting the resale shops and I've found some things I think you're really going to like. Let's try them on, shall we?" She teetered into his suite on her four-inch stilettos.

Jack closed the door and turned. "I appreciate your help and all but I've already got enough clothes for this gig."

"Well, then, you can use them on your next assignment." She started digging in the bag. "You're not going to believe some of the stuff I found. Theory pants. A Cavalli shirt that's to die for. You've got a whole new career going for you, Jackie, so you have to dress the part. You can't go tailing rich people into swanky places like this if you look like some kind of bum."

"Maybe you should have been a little more con-

cerned with the way I looked before you did this to my hair," he grumbled.

Cher rolled her eyes. "Why don't you just admit that you like it? If you didn't, you'd have been beating down my door by now to get me to fix it."

"You said you couldn't fix it, and besides, I've been a little preoccupied with a case, remember?"

Cher tried not to sound too interested. "Oh, yeah, how's that going?"

"It's going." He headed for the bedroom. "I need to get dressed. Just make yourself at home. I'll be right back."

"I'll do that," Cher murmured.

She waited until the door closed between them, then she turned and quickly surveyed the suite. The elaborate furnishings and ornate drapery weren't exactly to her taste, but she could adjust. Man, could she ever. It was high time she got a taste of the high life.

She opened the bar and glanced inside. Chivas, Cristall. There was even a bottle of Krug. Cher had never even seen a bottle of that stuff in person, let alone tasted it.

"So what *are* you going to do about my hair?" Jack called from the bedroom.

"I told you, I'll have to speak to my instructor about it." Of course, that wasn't going to happen now because unbeknownst to Jack, she'd dropped out of beauty school. With the ten-thousand dollar

check from the *National Intruder* burning a hole in her pocket, her options had suddenly become a whole lot more interesting.

"By the way, I've got enough money now to get my car back from the finance company," he said. "I won't have to impose on you for a ride anymore."

"No hurry," she said distractedly, still busy taking inventory of the bar. "My brother, Jerry, won't get off that oil rig for another two weeks." Of course, if her older brother ever found out that she'd borrowed his precious Corvette, he'd blow a gasket. But it didn't matter because if everything went according to plan, Cher would be long gone by the time he made landfall and checked his mileage.

Just as soon as the *Intruder*'s check cleared the bank, she was hightailing it out of there because, truth be told, she was more concerned about Jack's reaction than she was her brother's. If he ever found out she was selling information about Celeste Fortune to the tabloids, he'd do worse than blow a gasket. Cher shuddered to think what he might do.

So the minute that check cleared, she was buying herself a one-way ticket to L.A. or New York. Maybe Las Vegas. But first, she might even book herself into this place for a day or two, just to get a taste of how the other half lived.

"Your champagne, Miss Maynard." She glanced down her nose at the invisible waiter. "Why, thank

you, darling." She accepted the invisible glass and waltzed around the room.

A knock sounded on the door, halting her in mid-step. "You want me to get that, Jack?"

"Yeah, it's probably room service. I ordered up some coffee."

"Room service," Cher muttered as she headed for the door. Yeah, she could definitely get used to this life.

She drew back the door and came face-to-face with Celeste Fortune. Cher almost gasped in surprise. She'd never been that close to a celebrity before, and for a moment, her resentment was overshadowed by her awe. She even felt a prickle of guilt for what was about to hit the tabloids. *Actress Stalked by Ex-Cop.*

Cher stared openly at the woman, her natural curiosity getting the better of her. She'd seen pictures of Celeste Fortune in Jack's apartment, and had even sneaked a peek at a couple of his videos without his knowing. It was true what they said about lighting and makeup. On the big screen, Celeste Fortune was a beautiful woman, but in person…not so much.

Oh, she was attractive, Cher admitted grudgingly, in a more wholesome, healthy kind of way. In fact, she looked…extremely healthy. The girl had packed on some pounds since her last flick.

Celeste looked discomfited by the scrutiny. She folded her arms over her chest. "I'm sorry to disturb

you, but I'm…looking for Jack." Her gaze flicked over Cher.

She's curious about me, too, Cher thought. *She's wondering what I'm doing in Jackie's suite. If I didn't know better, I'd swear she seems jealous, but then that would mean…*

Cher's jaw dropped in astonishment. That would mean Celeste Fortune had fallen for Jack Fury. That would mean…oh, boy. That would mean she was in for one hellacious surprise when the *Intruder* hit the stands. Assuming, of course, that Jack still hadn't come clean with her. And Cher was willing to bet her ten-thousand-dollar windfall that he hadn't.

Well, now, didn't this just add a new twist to the story? Cher wondered suddenly how much more the tabloids would be willing to pay for this little tidbit. Celeste Fortune in love with her stalker. If Cher could get photos, the price might go as high as six figures, and then her options would really get interesting.

"Is he here?" Celeste asked.

"Jack?" Cher leaned against the door frame. "He's in the bedroom getting dressed. Want to come in and wait?"

Celeste's eyes widened slightly before she glanced away. She really was jealous. This just kept getting better and better.

"No, thanks," she said coolly.

Cher shrugged. "Suit yourself. Any message?"

"Just that…I'll talk to him later. No, on second thought, don't even mention that I was here. It's not important."

"Whatever you say." Cher closed the door just as Jack emerged from the bedroom wearing the new clothes she'd brought over. She gave a low whistle. "Would you look at that? They're a perfect fit."

"Thanks." He tugged at the shirt collar as he glanced around. "No coffee?"

"Uh, that wasn't room service."

"Who was it then?" He was still fiddling with his shirt.

"Celeste Fortune."

He glanced up sharply. "She was here? Why didn't she come in?"

Cher's gaze narrowed, taking in every nuance of his expression.

"Did she say what she wanted?" he demanded.

Cher shrugged. "Only that it wasn't important. You know something?" She paused. "Celeste Fortune doesn't look at all in person the way she looks in the movies."

"No, actually, she looks exactly the same," Jack murmured as he turned toward the door.

CASSIE HAD decided that she was not, under any circumstances, going to ask Jack about the woman in his hotel suite. She didn't want to sound needy and desperate and jealous by giving him the third degree.

Instead, when she saw him later that day, she tried to play it cool and sophisticated. So he'd had a woman in his room. A very attractive woman with a raspy, alluring voice. Big deal.

But as it turned out, Jack volunteered the information as they drove down to Bayside to pick up Mr. Bogart. Cher Maynard, he explained, was an old friend who'd decided to drop in and surprise him.

Oh, okay.

And by the time they were headed back to Houston an hour or so later, Cassie had just about decided to believe him. Except for one thing. If Jack really was an undercover agent for Interpol, how was it that an old friend had managed to find him so easily?

Unless, of course, she wasn't an old friend, but a colleague. Maybe Cher Maynard was also an agent, and she'd been assigned to Jack's case.

Yeah, that worked for Cassie. It made as much sense as anything else that had happened in the past few days. Besides, agent or not, Cher Maynard was the least of her worries.

She glanced at Jack's profile. He was scowling slightly at the road as they zipped northbound on the Gulf Freeway. She wondered what he was thinking because she could have sworn she'd seen suspicion in those blue eyes the night before. She could have sworn she'd heard hesitation in his voice when he called her Celeste. But she'd seen no evidence of his misgivings today. Whether he'd resolved his own

doubts or whether it was all an act, Cassie had no idea. One thing she was pretty sure of, though. Jack Fury had his own secrets.

So what was she doing falling for a guy like that? And Cassie was falling for him. She couldn't seem to help herself. He was just so *interesting.* And so attractive. So…quirky. He had all the qualities she found irresistible. And the fact that she didn't trust him completely, well, that only seemed to add to his appeal.

Tearing her gaze from his profile, she glanced over her shoulder. Mr. Bogart snoozed peacefully in the back seat. Although he and Jack's stepmother had apparently got along famously, his reaction upon seeing Cassie had been gratifying. He'd made a mad dash for her, wagging his tail furiously and sniffing her ankles. Then he'd done the same to Jack. Cassie had been amazed all over again how drawn the little dog was to him. She knew exactly how Mr. Bogart felt, and she wanted to believe that both their instincts couldn't be wrong.

Once they were back at the Mirabelle, Cassie clipped Mr. Bogart's leash to his collar and led him inside. He pranced through the lobby of the elegant hotel as if he owned the place. *You had to admire a guy with that kind of confidence,* Cassie thought.

No one was around in the lobby. It was late afternoon, too early for Lyle Lester to be on duty, which begged the question of how he might spend his time

off. But then, Cassie wasn't so certain she wanted to know. The man definitely gave off some weird vibes.

After they exited the elevator, Jack walked her to her suite. Cassie couldn't help remembering what had happened the last time he'd done that, and a part of her—a very big part—wanted a repeat performance.

"Would you like to come in?" she tried to ask casually as she inserted her key card into the lock.

"If you don't mind. I've been doing a little research, and I'd like to tell you what I found out."

Why hadn't he told her in the car?

Don't look a gift horse in the mouth, Cassie.

She closed the door and turned anxiously to Jack. "What?"

He nodded toward the elegant iron and glass table that had been placed in front of the French doors. "Let's sit first."

Once they were both settled at the table, Cassie folded her hands in her lap while Jack removed a notebook from his pocket and flipped it open. "We'll start with Lyle Lester."

She'd just been thinking about him. "Lyle? What about him?"

"I had one of my contacts here in Houston run his name through some of the national databases. Lester doesn't have a criminal record so I decided to Google him. You wouldn't believe how many hits his name produced."

"What kind of hits?" Cassie asked in surprise.

"He was an Olympic athlete, for one thing. A gymnast. And for a while, he was with Cirque du Soleil. But he only toured for a couple of years before sustaining an injury that forced him to retire."

"Wow," Cassie murmured in awe. Cirque du Soleil. Who would have thought? She loved those performances. Her estimation of Lyle Lester notched up a few degrees. "That explains his grace and agility. I thought he might have been a dancer."

"It also explains how he would be able to climb down an elevator shaft in the dark," Jack pointed out.

Cassie gasped. She hadn't even thought of that.

"I also placed a few calls to L.A." He flipped through his notebook, then glanced up. "I talked to your landlord. He said that your roommate has been AWOL for a couple of weeks. He wasn't too happy. Seems she skipped out on a month's rent."

Cassie frowned. "But I talked to her just a couple of days ago. She was still at the apartment then. Remember, I told you she said she found my itinerary on the computer. And she said that a man had been around asking questions about me. She even said he'd cornered her in the parking lot."

"Not in the parking lot at the apartments. At least not according to the landlord, and I don't think he was lying. The guy seemed pretty upset about that rent."

"But…why would she lie?"

Jack shrugged. "Probably because she didn't want you to know where she really was. For all we know, she could be right here in Houston."

Cassie's eyes widened. "You don't really think she's behind all this, do you? Blowing up the boat, ransacking Gold's beach house. Why would she do something like that?"

"It's like I told you yesterday. Resentment and jealousy are powerful motivations. According to her bio, she studied under one the most prestigious acting coaches in New York. He even touted her as the next Meryl Streep, but once she hit Hollywood, she couldn't land anything but bit parts. And there you were, an unsophisticated girl from nowhere whose star was on the rise. Until you got involved with Owen Fleming, that is."

Cassie cringed. "I don't want to talk about Owen Fleming."

"Then let's talk about his wife, shall we?" Jack turned another page in his notebook. "What do you know about Margo Fleming?"

"Only that, according to Mrs. Ambrose-Pritchard, she has ties to a Mafia family in Chicago."

"If she's connected to the Gambinis, it's a distant connection at best. But get this. Margo is Fleming's second wife. She was married to his partner when they first met, and he was still married to his first wife. They had a torrid affair, and the whole thing got pretty nasty. Sound familiar?"

Cassie didn't say anything, but inside she shuddered. The Hollywood lifestyle was appealing to her less and less.

The phone rang and when she made no move to answer it, Jack glanced up. "Are you going to get that?"

"Do I have to?"

"I think you'd better. It might be Vargas."

Cassie rose and crossed the room to answer, expecting Jack to follow her, but instead he remained seated, his blue gaze tracking her across the room.

"Hello?"

"Cassie?"

At the sound of her cousin's voice, Cassie whirled away from Jack's gaze, her hand gripping the phone. "I've been hoping you'd call," she tried to say lightly.

"Are you alone?"

Cassie's hand tightened on the phone. "No."

"Can you get rid of him?"

Him? How did she know it was a him? "I don't think so."

"Okay, then just take the phone into the bedroom. Tell him I'm your agent or something."

"Can't you call back later?" Cassie asked as she turned back to Jack. His gaze was so intense that her hand began to tremble. She forced a smile. "I'm…in the middle of something."

"This can't wait. I have to talk to you *now*, before

you do something crazy. It's a matter of life and death, Cass. Yours and mine."

A tremor went through Cassie at her cousin's urgent warning. She put her hand over the mouthpiece. "I'm sorry," she said to Jack. "But I'm going to have to take the call. It's…my agent. Something about a contract. I'll just be a minute." She headed toward the bedroom.

"Take your time," he said behind her, but Cassie wasn't sure he'd bought her explanation or not.

Inside the bedroom, she closed the door, then lifted the cordless phone to her ear. "What's going on, Sissy? Where the hell are you?"

"It doesn't matter where I am—"

"It matters to me!" Cassie bit her lip, trying to control her anger. With an effort, she lowered her voice. "Someone wants to kill you, and now they're after me."

"I know, I know. Things have gotten completely out of control—"

"What *things*?" Cassie demanded. Once again she had to struggle to keep her voice lowered. "There's a cop right outside my door. I'm going out there and tell him everything unless you give me one good reason why I shouldn't."

"No! Don't do that, Cassie! You start talking, you could get us both killed."

"As opposed to just me?" Cassie lashed out.

"You don't understand. It's all been carefully set

up. All carefully planned. You've been in no real danger."

"Uh, you don't call an exploding boat 'real danger'?"

"That was…unfortunate. We miscalculated—"

"What do you mean, *we?* Celeste, what is going on? Who's in this with you? Owen?"

Celeste paused. "Forget about Owen. He's no longer in the picture."

"What about his diamond? Is that in the picture?"

Her cousin's voice altered subtly. "What diamond? What are you talking about?"

"The three-million-dollar ring he gave you. Don't tell me a rock like that has slipped your mind. Wait a minute," Cassie said slowly, as she had a sudden flash. "That's what all this is about, isn't it? If that diamond gets stolen, you collect on the insurance. It all makes sense now. The exploding boat. The ransacked beach house. I just don't understand where I fit into the picture. Unless you somehow plan for me to take the fall—"

"Cassie, shut up and just listen, okay? It's not what you think. It has nothing to do with the diamond. Do you understand? It's so much more than that. I can't go into it right now, but I need you to trust me. And I need you to keep your mouth shut. Just for a little longer."

"If you want me to trust you, then tell me where you are."

"I can't do that. Not yet. It would ruin everything. Please, just trust me."

"Damn it, Celeste—"

"I know it's asking a lot, but I swear I'll find a way to make it up to you."

"If I'm still alive," Cassie muttered.

"You won't get hurt. Not as long as you stick close to Jack Fury."

Cassie gasped. "What do you know about Jack Fury? Is he in this with you?"

"We've never met. But I'm told he's the best at what he does." She paused again. "You've got a thing for him, don't you?"

The question startled Cassie. How could her cousin possibly have known that?

"Listen to me, Cass. If you do anything to screw this up, Jack walks out of your life. But if you keep your mouth shut and let it play out, we can all end up with what we want."

"And just what is it you want—"

But it was too late. The line had gone dead.

Chapter Thirteen

After Jack left her suite, Cassie didn't see him for the rest of the day, although he did call once after he'd left her room to tell her that he was following up on some leads. He also cautioned her to keep her door locked and not to let anyone into her suite.

Should that warning include him? Cassie wondered.

Because, try as she might, she couldn't get her cousin's cryptic remarks out of her head. *"We've never met. But I'm told he's the best at what he does."*

And just what was it that he did?

"Listen to me, Cass. If you do anything to screw this up, Jack walks out of your life. But if you keep your mouth shut and let it play out, we can all end up getting what we want."

What had she meant by that? Were she and Jack in some kind of conspiracy? Some kind of con? And

if they were, what exactly was their game? Did it have something to do with the diamond?

Cassie's head spun with all the possibilities. More than once she picked up the phone to call Jack and tell him about her cousin's call, but she couldn't quite make herself follow through with it because something else Celeste had said kept niggling at her. *"You start talking, you could get us both killed."*

What if her cousin was right? What if their safety depended on Cassie's silence?

But how could she trust Celeste after everything that had happened?

How could she trust Jack? Or anyone for that matter?

What the hell had she gotten herself into?

Finally, after hours of useless speculation, Cassie ordered room service, hoping a good meal might help clear her head. But once the food arrived, she discovered she didn't have an appetite—unusual for her—and decided instead to take a long bath. But even after a hot soak, she was still as wound up as ever.

Slipping into a pair of silk pajamas, she lay down on the bed and began to channel surf, finally lighting on the ten o'clock news.

She listened idly as the anchor glided seamlessly from a suicide bombing story in the Middle East to

a piece on Medicare reform and then finally to a local homicide.

Cassie shot up in bed when she heard the name of the victim. "…the body of a man found in the trunk of a car at Bush Intercontinental Airport earlier today has been identified as Hollywood film producer Owen Fleming. No word yet as to how long Fleming's body had been in the trunk, but records show that he flew into Houston a week ago. Investigators are now trying to piece together Fleming's movements on the day of his arrival. Viewers may recall that Fleming made headlines a few weeks ago when his affair with actress Celeste Fortune became public. A spokesperson for the actress says that she's in seclusion and can't be reached for comment. Fortune is just one of many witnesses the police want to question in connection to Fleming's death, including his wife whose whereabouts are unknown."

The anchor went to another story and Cassie sat in stunned silence, her heart pounding so hard she thought for a moment she might actually be having an attack.

Owen Fleming was dead. He'd been murdered in Houston. And the police wanted to question Celeste.

And when they came looking for her, they'd find Cassie.

Dear lord, she *was* being set up! No wonder Celeste had urged Cassie to keep quiet for a little while longer. If she waited to come forward until after the

body was found, it would look like she was trying to cover her tracks.

They might even have planted evidence to incriminate her. Hairs or fibers at the crime scene or on his body that could be traced back to her!

Her heart still racing, Cassie jumped out of bed, grabbed her key card, and ran out of the suite. Still in a panic, she pounded on Jack's door, and when he finally answered, she rushed past him without waiting for an invitation.

"I don't know who you are or why you're here. I don't even know if I can trust you, but I've got no one else to turn to," she said desperately after he'd closed the door. "They're setting me up, Jack. I could go to prison for life. I could be executed. Oh, God, If you're in on this—"

He crossed the distance between them in two strides and took hold of her arms. "In on what? What are you talking about? What's happened?"

"You don't know?" Cassie glanced frantically around the room. "You haven't been watching the news?"

"I just got out of the shower."

Out of the shower? Suddenly, Cassie realized that he was standing before her in nothing but a towel. It was slung low around his waist, revealing a lean, hard, muscular expanse of tanned skin.

For a moment, the fear storming through her came

to a standstill, and Cassie let her gaze travel over him. He looked good enough to—

Focus, Cassie! You're in big trouble.

The tempest began to churn inside her head again, and she shuddered. "I don't want to go to prison, Jack."

His grip on her tightened. "Nobody's going to prison. Just calm down and tell me what happened."

"They found Owen Fleming's body stuffed in the trunk of his car at the airport. He was murdered, and the police are going to want to question me about it. But I didn't do anything wrong. You have to believe me. I can't tell the police anything because *I'm not Celeste.*" There. She'd finally said it. She'd blurted it out, and now she bit her lip, waiting for Jack's reaction.

For a split second, he didn't say anything. Then his gaze narrowed. "You're the cousin. The one you told me about. Cassie."

Her eyes widened as she stared up at him. "How did you know that unless…you've known all along, haven't you? You *are* in on it."

She tried to back away, but his grasp on her arms held fast. "I'm not in on anything. I saw Celeste at Ethan Gold's house last night."

Cassie gasped. "Why didn't you tell me?"

His expression hardened. "Because I wanted to find out what kind of scam you two were trying to pull." He released her then, but Cassie didn't move away.

She put a hand to the side of her face. "If Celeste was at Ethan's place, then that must mean they're working together. That must mean… Jack, do you think they got rid of poor Owen…the same way they got rid of Ethan's wife?"

"That's jumping to a pretty big conclusion, but anything's possible."

Cassie turned away and started to pace. "That's why he threatened me so that I wouldn't go to the police. They couldn't have me spilling the beans before the body was found."

"Wait a minute?" Jack grabbed her arm. "You talked to Gold? When?"

"He came to the car last night while you were at his house."

"And you didn't tell me?" His fingers tightened on her arms. "Why the hell not?"

"Ouch." Cassie drew back even though he hadn't really hurt her.

"Sorry," he said contritely, "but why didn't you tell me you'd talked to Gold?"

"I couldn't. He said that if I told you, if I told anyone, he'd go to the police and tell them who I really am. Without Celeste's corroboration, they could throw me in jail for fraud and identity theft and who knows what all. I was afraid to tell you because I thought you might not believe me. You could have

just turned me into the police without listening to my side of things. And because…I didn't quite trust you."

His scowl deepened at that. "Have I done anything to make you think you can't trust me?" he demanded.

"…no."

"I'm here for only one reason—to protect you. Do you believe that?"

"Yes, but…do you believe me?"

"I believe you and Celeste cooked up some kind of scam and that things somehow got out control. I don't believe you killed Owen Fleming, but I think you're in over your head. You'd better come clean with me, Celeste—Cassie…whatever the hell your name is, and you'd better do it now."

Cassie nodded. "You're right. Of course, you're right. It's time for the truth." She knew she was babbling, but couldn't seem to stop. "It all started a few weeks ago, just after Celeste's affair with Owen became public. Everyone in Hollywood was talking about it. Celeste was being hounded by the paparazzi so she decided to get out of town for a while. When her publicist suggested she get a decoy, she called me because we'd always resembled one another. She said she'd booked a suite here at the Mirabelle and that all I had to do was stay here and pretend to be her. That way, if any paparazzi followed her to Houston, they'd see that she was here alone."

Jack's expression turned skeptical. "Why didn't she just stay here herself?"

"She didn't say, but I figured it was because she planned to go away with Owen."

"And now he's been murdered," Jack said grimly.

Cassie shuddered. "A month in a luxury hotel, she said. Room service. My own Jacuzzi. A chance for me to get away from—"

"The jilted fiancé?"

Was that disapproval she heard in his voice? Cassie frowned. "You have to understand how it was for me. The Cantrells were making my life miserable in Manville—that's where I'm from, Manville, Louisiana. It's just across the state line. But that's not the only reason I agreed to Celeste's proposal." Cassie turned, suddenly unable to face Jack's accusing gaze. "I just…needed to be someone else for a while. Someone glamorous and exciting. Someone who wouldn't be afraid of a little adventure. But then all these awful things started happening. The boat. The beach house. That night in the elevator. And now this."

"I don't understand. Why didn't you tell me the truth after the boat exploded? You must have known then you were in danger."

Cassie turned back. "Because I wasn't sure I could trust you, and because…I liked the excitement, the attention. A part of me even liked the danger. I know that sounds crazy, but you have to understand

what my life was like before. My mother was sick for nearly ten years. There was no one to take care of her but me. I know that makes me sound like a do-gooder in your book, but it wasn't like that. I had my days when I resented my predicament, sure. There were plenty of times when I wanted to get in my car and just keep driving. But I didn't because she was my mother and I loved her. But…" Cassie closed her eyes briefly. "I don't know if you've ever seen anyone after the ravages of lung cancer, but it's a terrible way to die. And a terrible thing to watch."

"I'm sorry, Cassie."

His words brought quick tears. "It's okay. Life goes on. And I guess that's why after she passed away, I was in a hurry to get on with my life. When Danny proposed, it seemed like a natural step to take. Start a new life, have a family of my own. But then when it came right down to it, I couldn't do it. I wasn't ready to be…committed again. To have commitments. I couldn't see living the rest of my life in Manville. So when Celeste called, I didn't question her about her motives because I didn't care. I just wanted out. And now I could go to prison. Or worse."

She blinked furiously, trying to hold back the tears, and to her surprise, Jack put his arms around her and pulled her close. "You're not going to prison. I promise you that."

Cassie melted against him and sighed. "I love it when you do that."

"Do what?" His lips whispered against her hair.

She sighed again. "Go all protective."

"I am going to protect you, Cassie. I'm not going to let anything happen to you."

"But…" She looked up at him. "You came here because of Celeste. And now that you know I'm not her…"

"What?"

"I just wish you could look at me the way you looked at me when you thought I was her. But I'm not glamorous. I'm not exciting. I'm just plain old Cassie Boudreaux, and now that you know that, you probably want nothing to do with me."

His arms tightened around her. "Do you remember what happened in the hallway outside your door last night?"

"You…kissed me."

"I kissed *you*. I already knew you weren't Celeste. I even thought you might be playing me, but I kissed you, anyway, because I couldn't help myself."

Cassie shivered as a dark look suddenly came into his eyes. "Really?" She slid her hand down his bare chest.

Jack caught her hand. "Are you sure you want to do that?"

She was sure, all right. Cassie had never been

more certain of anything in her life. "When all this is over, there's a good chance we'll never see each other again. You'll go on to your next assignment, and I'll…I don't know what I'm going to do."

"Cassie, there's something—"

She pressed a fingertip to his lips. "Don't talk."

And so he didn't. He didn't say a word even when she curled her fingers around the towel and pulled it free.

To Jack's utter delight and surprise, Cassie Boudreaux had no inhibitions in the bedroom. None whatsoever. She gave as good as she got, and she wasn't the least bit shy in telling him exactly what she wanted.

And Jack had no problem in fulfilling her every demand. He undressed her, kissing her slowly and deeply as the silk fabric slid to the floor. Then he carried her to the bed where she lay naked and writhing as he explored every inch of her body with his hands and his lips and his tongue.

She was one gorgeous woman, and her obvious enjoyment of what they were doing only heightened Jack's own pleasure. He took his time with her, teasing her to the brink and then prolonging the ecstasy for as long as he could until her release seemed to burst along her every nerve ending. In the throes of passion, she clutched at the sheet, gasping for breath, and then she plunged her fingers into his hair and

drew him up to her. He held her for a long time until her shudders subsided, and then she began to make love to him.

Her hair fell across her face as she bent over him, kissing her way down his chest and along his abdomen, drawing a sharp gasp from him as she moved even lower, teasing him with her tongue.

And then she got serious. Jack thought he was going to explode. He'd never had anything feel so good and knew that he had to stop her before it was too late.

"Damn, you're good at that," he said in wonder.

She lifted her head. "I know."

Her smile almost sent him over the edge. She was completely guileless in bed. Jack wasn't sure he'd ever met anyone quite like her, and he knew it was going to be a long time before he'd forget her.

They kissed, their tongues tangling in desperate passion as she straddled him and joined their bodies in an even more intimate way.

His hands on her hips, he tried to set the rhythm, but who was he kidding? Cassie was in charge, and she knew exactly what she was doing.

And then it was she who tried to prolong the ecstasy, lifting and settling herself over him so slowly and so deeply that Jack felt as if each thrust would be his last. But somehow he hung on. Somehow he managed to wait until her movements became more

frantic, more desperate, and when she began to shudder, only then did he let go.

He held her still, letting the sensations rush over him. Then he pulled her to him and wrapped his arms around her.

After a few moments, Cassie stirred.

"That…was incredible," she murmured. She got up then and walked slowly to the bathroom, pausing at the door to glance over her shoulder. She didn't say a word, but her smile spoke volumes.

AFTER THEY'D showered, they went back to bed. Cassie only meant to lie down for a moment, but she dozed off almost immediately, and when she awakened, it was after midnight. She put her hand on Jack's shoulder and gave him a shake.

"Jack? I forgot about Mr. Bogart. I have to go take him out. Poor thing's probably about to burst."

He rolled over and slung an arm over his face. "What?"

"I have to go take Mr. Bogart for a walk."

He opened one eye. "Uh, I don't think that's Mr. Bogart."

"What are you talking about?" *He must be still half asleep,* Cassie thought.

"I think I saw the real Mr. Bogart with Celeste at Ethan Gold's place. You have a decoy."

"What?" Cassie sat up in outrage. "You mean

this whole time I've been catering to that damn dog, treating him as if he was my own…" She kept right on grumbling as she swung her legs over the side of the bed and reached for her pajamas. "Well I'll tell you one thing. Whoever Sam belongs to, they're not getting him back. He's mine now."

"Sam? Let me guess. As in Sam Spade?"

"He did find that blood at Gold's beach house, didn't he?"

Jack lifted himself on his elbows and watched her dress. "Give me a minute to throw on some clothes and I'll come with you."

Good. Cassie had been hoping he'd say that. "I'll go get him and meet you back here."

She retrieved her key from the living room where she'd dropped it earlier and left Jack's suite. Unlocking her door, she stepped inside, then called the dog.

When he didn't respond, she thought he must be sleeping. Cassie walked into the bedroom and flipped on the light. His little bed was empty, and she started to panic. "Sam? Mr. Bogart? Whoever you are?"

Then she heard him whimper and she spun. The bathroom door was closed. She was almost certain she'd left it open earlier.

A shiver crawled up Cassie's spine. Someone had been in her suite. She was almost certain of it. What

if the intruder was still there, hiding in the bathroom with the dog?

She turned to the door, intent on making a run for it, but the whimper grew louder. Then he began to paw frantically at the door.

There was no way Cassie could leave him. Shoving her own fear aside, she hurried across the room and drew open the door. He came running out, and Cassie knelt to scoop him up in her arms. "Come on, boy. We've got to get out of here."

The dog began to yelp furiously then, and his eyes widened as he peered at something over her shoulder. Someone had come up behind them. Without making a sound…

Clutching the dog in her arms, Cassie spun. He was there, just inside the bedroom, an armed intruder with a dark mask pulled over his face. Another one came in behind him. Slowly, they started toward Cassie.

She backed toward the bathroom. If she could get inside, lock the door—

They were quicker than that. They sprang across the room and grabbed her, and when she tried to scream, a hand clamped over her mouth.

"Shut that damn dog up," the one holding her said.

The other one took the Chihuahua and put him

back in the bathroom. Cassie could hear the frantic dog yelping behind the closed door.

"Hurry up," the first one muttered, "Before that cop comes to investigate."

"Maybe I want him to come," the second one said. There was something eerily familiar about his voice. Cassie shuddered at the sound. "Maybe I've got some unfinished business with him, too."

Cassie had been struggling the whole time, but now she went suddenly still. *No!* It couldn't be—

"Maybe I want to teach him what happens when he touches Danny Cantrell's woman."

Oh, God, it *was* him! It was Danny! The Cantrells had somehow found her. They were the ones who'd been terrorizing her!

Celeste hadn't set her up after all. Her cousin hadn't even been the target. Cassie was.

And now she recognized the second man's voice as well. It was Danny's Uncle Earl.

Cassie had known they were vindictive, but she hadn't realized they were so dangerous. And cunning.

Fear ripped through her at what they might do to her, and she renewed her struggles, biting the fleshy hand that held her mouth. Earl Cantrell merely cursed and tightened his grip. "Stupid bitch bit me."

"Don't call her that."

"Sorry," the older man muttered. "Just stick her

with that damn needle and let's get the hell out of here."

"Hold her still, then."

Cassie felt a sharp prick in her arm, and almost instantly she went limp. She couldn't walk or speak, but she wasn't completely unconscious. She had a vague sense of being carried through the suite, of the night air on her face as they hurried through the French doors to the balcony. And then she had the terrifying sensation of hanging in midair by a rope as she was slowly lowered to the ground.

THE DOOR to Cassie's suite was ajar when Jack got there. He supposed she'd left it open for him, but he knocked, anyway. When there was no answer, he pushed the door open and stuck his head inside. "Cassie?"

He knew at once that something was wrong. Pulling his weapon, he walked into the suite and glanced around. "Cassie?"

Then he heard a sound coming from the other room, and he let out a breath of relief. She was probably just freshening up.

He went through the bedroom and knocked on the bathroom door. "Cassie? You in there?"

As the sound of his voice, Sam began to bark excitedly, and Jack threw open the door. The little dog

was so happy to see him that he practically threw himself into Jack's arms.

"Where's Cassie? Where'd she go, boy?"

"I think I can answer that."

The voice startled him, and Jack whipped around, weapon drawn, but he was too late. Max Tripp had already gotten the drop on him.

Chapter Fourteen

When Cassie first opened her eyes, the room spun so fast she thought she was going to be sick. She lay perfectly still, not daring to move a muscle until the dizziness passed. Then she lifted herself on her elbows and glanced around.

She had no idea where she was. She could only make out vague shapes in the room. A dresser. A chest of drawers. A second bed.

And someone was on that bed. Cassie gasped as a human shape took form.

Slowly, she got to her feet, swaying to and fro for a moment until she finally got her balance. Then she crossed the room and leaned over the other bed.

The woman lay on her back, and in the dim light shining in through a window, Cassie could just make out her features. It was Celeste.

"Sissy?" When there was no response, Cassie put her hand on her cousin's shoulder and gave her a gentle shake. "Celeste?"

Still no response. Panic welled up in her throat. Was her cousin still alive?

Cassie knew she had to get help. Willing away the fog still clouding her brain, she got up and went over to the door. She could hear voices in the next room, but instead of calling out, she pressed her ear to the door and listened for a moment.

"…take her into the swamp and dump her," a woman was saying. "Make sure no one finds the body. You can do whatever you want with the other one."

"Now wait just a minute," Earl Cantrell drawled. "We didn't sign up for no murder."

There was a slight hesitation, and then the woman said, "Does this ease your conscience?"

Earl whistled. "Yes, ma'am, it surely does. But this here transaction will have to be between you and me. Don't say nuthin' to the boy. Danny wouldn't go for it."

"You can tell your nephew whatever you like. Just make that woman go way, permanently. Understand?"

"Oh, I understand all right."

"Good. Are they both still out."

"Won't come to for hours."

"What about Ethan Gold? He didn't see you, did he?"

"He didn't see nuthin'. He never even knew what hit him."

"Wonderful. Now, if you don't mind, I'd like to see them."

"Help yourself."

Cassie scurried across the room and lay down on the bed. When the door opened, she closed her eyes and held her breath. There was no sound for several long seconds, then she heard someone walk across the room. When the footsteps moved away from her, she opened her eyes and watched through her lashes.

A tiny woman stood over the other bed, staring down at Celeste. Then she bent, picked up Celeste's limp hand, and viciously removed the huge ring that glittered on her left hand. She held the diamond in her palm for a moment before squeezing her fist around it. Then turning, she exited the room without looking back.

The moment the door clicked shut, Cassie was on her feet. She hurried over to Celeste and shook her shoulders again, this time not so gently. "Celeste, wake up! We have to get out of here!"

Celeste moaned.

"That's it! Come on. You can do it. Just open your eyes."

But no matter how much she urged or how hard she shook her, Cassie couldn't rouse her cousin. But at least she now knew that Celeste was alive. And the Boudreauxs did not go down without a fight.

Making her way over to the window, Cassie glanced out. Moonlight glistened on water, and she could see a boat tied up at the end of a small, wooden dock. She knew where they were. Minnie Cantrell's place. Right smack in the middle of a swamp. Which meant an escape could include gators and cotton-mouths.

Cassie shivered. She'd always hated coming out here with Danny. The house was old and creaky, and the air always smelled of the swamp. Of dark places and darker secrets. But at least she'd pinpointed their location, and even though Cassie wasn't exactly in her element, she could navigate her way out of the swamp if she had to.

She tried to open the window, but the sash wouldn't budge. It had either been nailed or painted shut, and Cassie doubted she could get it open without a crowbar. That left breaking the windows—

Someone was coming. Cassie rushed back to the bed and stretched out just as Earl Cantrell came in. He walked straight over to Celeste, picked her up and slung her over his shoulder. When he turned back to the door, Cassie grabbed the only weapon she could find—a ceramic lamp on the bedside table—and swung it against his skull as hard as she could.

But that damned Cantrell sixth sense must have warned him of the danger because he moved at ex-

actly the right moment, and the lamp only struck a glancing below. He whirled, and Cassie wasn't so lucky. His fist caught her underneath the chin, and she went down without a sound.

WHEN CASSIE CAME TO, the dizziness was back. Tentatively, she touched her chin. They must have drugged her again, because she felt no pain. Nor could she do much more than lift herself on her elbows to glance around. She was lying on the same bed as before, but instead of her pajamas, she was now wearing a wedding dress. *Her* wedding dress.

The blood iced in her veins as she took in the yards and yards of tulle billowing around her. She thought she must be in the middle of a nightmare, but then Minnie Cantrell came over and peered down at her. "You're awake, are you?" She turned and said over her shoulder, "You boys get over here and help her to her feet."

Two more Cantrells appeared and took Cassie's arms. One on each side, they lifted her to her feet, then hauled her toward the door. Cassie wanted to resist, but she couldn't. She couldn't seem to make her arms and legs move on her own, and her tongue was so thick she could do little more than groan.

They half carried, half dragged her down the long, narrow corridor to the front of the house. When they

appeared in the doorway to the living room, the wedding march began to play.

Cassie glanced around. The room was full of Cantrells. Cousins. Aunts and uncles. All of them dressed in their Sunday finest and staring at her expectantly.

Oh, my God, Cassie thought in horror. *They're here for a wedding.*

Hers.

And Danny's.

He stood at the front of the room underneath an archway of flowers, waiting for her. He nodded, and the two cousins brought her forward.

This couldn't be happening. He didn't actually expect her to marry him, did he? He couldn't force her into matrimony, could it?

But that was exactly what he planned to do.

When Cassie was brought to his side, he put his arm around her waist to support her. The two cousins melted away.

The man officiating gave her a strange look. "Miss? Are you okay?"

No, I'm not okay. You have to help me.

Cassie opened her mouth, but to her horror, nothing came out.

"She's feeling a little under the weather," Danny explained. He squeezed her waist. "We did a little too much celebrating last night, didn't we, darlin'?" He gave the justice of the peace a wink.

"Are you sure she's well enough to continue? Maybe you should postpone—"

"There's not going to be any postponement," Danny said. "Not this time. I've been waiting long enough, so just get on with it. These folks came here expecting a wedding, and that's what they're going to get."

"If that's what you want." The man cleared his throat and began in a solemn tone, "Dearly beloved, we are gathered here—"

"Just get to the good part," Danny cut in.

The justice of the peace looked slightly taken aback by the whole proceeding, but the Cantrells' reputation preceded them. Cassie could just imagine what must be going through the poor man's head. He had a family and a reputation to uphold. He was a pillar in the community and might even have a future in politics ahead of him, but all that could be taken away by one of Minnie Cantrell's hexes. "If anyone objects, stand up now or forever hold your peace—"

The front door burst open, and all heads turned. A few of the women even gasped. Jack stood poised in the doorway, weapon drawn, eyes blazing with fury.

Cassie's knees threatened to collapse, and not just from the effects of the drug.

"I object," he said.

Get him out of here!" Danny screamed. But when

a couple of the men started toward Jack, he cocked his gun and they backed off, holding their hands in the air.

"Everyone, just stay right where you are." He glanced at Cassie, and the look in his eyes made her heart beat even harder. "Are you all right?"

She nodded.

"Can you walk on your own?"

When she didn't answer, Jack said to Danny, "Bring her to me."

"Like hell—"

"Kidnapping is a federal offense. The FBI's been called, and in the meantime, the local boys are on their way out here. If you don't want to make it any worse on yourself than it already is, just let us walk out of here right now."

His words seemed to have an effect, or maybe it was the gun. Whatever the reason, Danny walked Cassie back down the aisle to Jack. "You're welcome to her," he muttered. "Bitch is more trouble than she's worth."

Outside, Cassie stumbled, and Jack caught her up in his arms. She clutched his shirt front. "Celeste…" she managed to croak. "Swamp…"

"Celeste is fine. We found her in time."

"Mrs. Ambrose…Pritchard…"

"Aka Margo Fleming," Jack said. "She used to be Evelyn Ambrose when she was married to her first husband. She changed it when she married Fleming."

In the car, Cassie collapsed against the door.

"Are you sure you're okay?" Jack asked anxiously.

Cassie nodded. "Thanks," she whispered.

"Any time." His gaze flicked over. "Nice dress, by the way."

JACK WANTED to take her to the hospital, but Cassie, who was feeling stronger by the minute, insisted on going to city hall where Celeste had gone to give her statement.

The moment Cassie walked through the door, her cousin jumped up and ran over to her. "Thank God, you're okay! I've been so worried about you!" Then she threw her arms around Cassie's neck, and Cassie was so surprised by the action that she didn't say anything at first.

Then, when Celeste pulled away, she murmured, "I'm glad you're okay, too."

"Thanks to your Mr. Fury. And Max." Celeste reached around and took the hand of the man standing behind her. Cassie glanced at him curiously. He was around thirty, tall and good-looking in a serious, conservative sort of way.

"I'm Max Tripp." He extended his hand to Cassie.

"I know you must have a lot of questions," Celeste said, "And I'll try to explain everything to you, but first…" She motioned to a small wooden table and chairs across the room. "Let's sit down, shall we?"

Once they were all settled, Cassie glanced at Jack.

He had been strangely quiet during the exchange. She wondered what was going on inside his head.

"First let me tell you that Margo has confessed to everything," Celeste said. Even after her ordeal, she still managed to look incredibly beautiful. And she had Max Tripp's undivided attention. He couldn't take his eyes off her.

And Jack? Was that the reason for his silence? Was he comparing Cassie to Celeste?

"She killed Owen and she tried to kill me," Celeste was saying.

Cassie wanted to feel compassion for her cousin, but at the moment, mostly what she felt was resentment. She wasn't proud of the emotion, but there it was. "That's why you wanted me to pretend to be you, isn't it? You knew someone was trying to kill you."

"You have every reason to be upset with me, Cassie, but you have to believe me. I never thought you'd be in any real danger." She looked very earnest saying that, but Cassie wasn't convinced.

"Then why the ruse?" she demanded.

Celeste and Max exchanged a glance. Then Celeste bit her lip. "I think I'd better go back to the beginning."

"Yes, why don't you do that?" Cassie agreed.

Her angry tone seemed to throw Celeste. Honestly, did she think Cassie was going to be thrilled by everything that had happened?

"It all started after my affair with Owen became

public." She paused and glanced down at her hands, as if overcome with shame. "Suddenly, I went from being a relatively obscure actress to having my picture splashed across all the tabloids. The paparazzi camped out on my doorstep night and day trying to catch me with Owen. It started wearing on my nerves. And then...I began to get phone calls. Hang ups at first, and then the caller started making nasty accusations. Threats. The harassment went on for weeks until I decided to leave town. That's when I called Max."

Jack sat forward suddenly. "*You* called Max?"

She nodded. "I've known him for a long time. We met in college, in fact. I knew he'd become a cop after graduation, and I heard through a mutual friend that he'd opened a private investigation firm. I thought if anyone could help me, he could."

"Help you do what?" Cassie asked.

"Find out who my harasser was. I suspected Margo, of course, but I couldn't prove it. And without proof, I had no leverage against her."

Another glance passed between her and Max, and then he took over the explanation. "We were fairly certain that if Margo was behind the threats, she wouldn't give up just because Celeste left town. We figured she'd follow her here. So we decided to set a trap."

"With me as bait." Cassie couldn't believe how gullible she'd been.

"Like I said, I never thought you'd be in any real danger," Celeste said. "Not with Jack watching over you."

Cassie turned, her heart suddenly in her throat. "You were in on this, too?" she asked in a wounded tone.

His eyes glinted with anger. "No. I was as much in the dark as you. It seems we've both been played."

"What do you mean?"

"Jack works for me," Max said.

Cassie swiveled back around to Jack. "But I thought…you said you worked for Interpol. That was just a lie, wasn't it? I must be the biggest fool in the world." She glanced away, then her gaze swung back to his. "Who are you?"

He shrugged. "Just an unemployed ex-cop."

"Unemployed?" She nodded toward Max. "He said you worked for him."

"Not any more," Jack said grimly.

"We'll talk about that later," Max said. "You see, Cassie, my business is not exactly your run-of-the-mill P.I. firm. I'll let Jack explain the details to you later, but suffice it to say that his assignment was to keep an eye on you. Find out everything he could about you. I knew you couldn't be in better hands. Jack was the best cop I ever worked with, and he's like a dog with a bone when he's working a case. All I had to do was arrange for him to see someone trying to break into your suite one night. Knowing him the way I do, I knew he'd move heaven and earth to keep you safe."

"So you just made all that up about the diamond and the jewel thief." A part of her had known that all along, but in light of Celeste's deception, Jack's betrayal suddenly seemed like the last straw. Cassie felt like a fool, and she hated it.

"I needed a cover," Jack said. "After the boat exploded that day, I had to come up with a reason to stay near you."

"Why didn't you just tell the truth?"

He shrugged. "Why didn't you?"

She lifted her chin. "I explained that last night."

Last night. Cassie had almost forgotten what had happened between her and Jack the night before, but now it came rushing back. Every passionate detail.

She blushed and glanced away.

"I suspected my roommate was the one feeding information to Margo so I set her up," Celeste said. "I deliberately left my itinerary where Olivia would find it, and sure enough, Margo came to Houston and checked herself into the Mirabelle to wait for me."

"Only she found me instead."

"According to her, she knew all along you were an imposter."

"Then why did she try to kill me? Why did she blow up Ethan Gold's boat? She was behind it, wasn't she?" Cassie asked doubtfully.

Celeste lifted her shoulders. "I suppose in her twisted way, she thought she could draw me out of hiding."

"There are still some things that don't make sense to me," Jack said. "If Margo Fleming was behind everything, why did Ethan Gold act so guilty? Why did he run away that day at the beach house when he saw us? And why did he threaten Cassie?"

"He ran because he wanted to get back to Houston and warn me about what had happened. But, unfortunately, Margo had him followed. She found out where I was staying, and that's when she got in touch with the Cantrells. Once she figured out you and I had swapped places, Cassie, it was a simple matter for her detectives to find out who you were and that you had a jilted fiancé in your past who might be willing to strike a bargain in exchange for your whereabouts." Celeste let out a long breath. "And the rest you know."

"There's still one thing you haven't explained to my satisfaction," Cassie said. "You say you came to Houston to lay a trap for Margo. If you truly thought there was no real danger, why not use yourself as bait?"

Color tinged Celeste's cheeks and she glanced away.

"Oh, I get it," Cassie said. "You didn't just come here to set a trap. You came here to meet Owen. That's why he was in Houston. He came here to see you."

"We were going away together." Celeste put a hand to her mouth, choking back sudden emotion. "With you already here pretending to be me, we knew

it would buy us some time with the paparazzi. We were going to use the evidence we gathered against Margo as leverage to get her to agree to a divorce."

"So she murdered him."

A tear rolled down Celeste's cheek, and Max handed her a handkerchief, which she accepted gratefully.

"I don't know about you," Jack muttered. "But I could use some air."

The sound of Celeste's quiet sobbing followed them out of the room. At the door, Cassie glanced back. Max Tripp had folded Celeste in his arms and was holding her close.

And Cassie could see from his expression that he was already madly, passionately, desperately in love with her.

Poor devil.

Outside, Cassie sank down on the steps, her voluminous skirts billowing all around her.

"So what did you think of that little performance?" Jack sat down beside her.

"You think it was all an act?" Cassie asked in surprise.

"Who knows?" He shrugged. "I'll tell you what I do think. No matter how she tries to sugarcoat it, she set you up, Cassie. She knew someone was after her, and she deliberately put you in the line of fire. She wasn't trying to bait a trap. She was trying to save her own butt."

"I feel like the biggest idiot in the world," Cassie said.

"You're not an idiot."

"No?" She studied the street. "I believed you, didn't I?"

"I didn't lie about the important things," he said softly. "I did want to protect you."

"So why didn't you just tell me the truth?"

"I wanted to. When I saw someone trying to break into your suite that night, I went to Max and told him we had to tell you everything. We had to warn you that you were in danger. I even threatened to go to the cops."

"Why didn't you?"

He rested his forearms on his knees as he watched the street. "Because I knew I couldn't get anyone at police headquarters to listen to me. I didn't exactly leave the department on amicable terms."

Cassie gave him a curious glance. "What do you mean?"

"I didn't quit. I was fired."

Her eyes widened in shock. "Why?"

"You remember that criminal psychologist you saw on TV talking about the Casanova case? She said there was an HPD detective who still believes the killer is out there somewhere. That cop was me, Cassie."

She shook her head in confusion. "How did that get you fired?"

"I kept investigating after we had a conviction. I knew the wrong man had been sent to prison, and I set out to prove it."

"They fired you because of that?" she asked incredulously.

"It's called insubordination." His gaze was still on the street. His voice had gone hard when he talked about the police department, and Cassie suspected he still hadn't come to terms yet with the fact that he was no longer a cop.

"What did you do after they let you go?"

"I continued to investigate for as long as I could, but eventually my savings ran out. My resources dried up. That's why I took the job with Max. Without funds, my investigation was at a standstill."

"That's admirable, Jack, but it sounds—"

"Obsessive?" He frowned. "So I've been told."

"I was going to say dedicated," she murmured.

He turned at that. "I promised those women justice, Cassie, and I won't rest until they have it."

Something in his eyes made Cassie shiver. She'd never seen this side of him before. "Why?"

"It's…complicated. My mother was murdered when I was thirteen. Her killers were never found, and it nearly tore our family apart. Betty helped save us, but it was something none of us ever got over. I promised myself a long time ago I'd do everything

in my power to keep other families from having to go through what we did."

"That's why Max said he knew you'd move heaven and earth to protect me," she said softly.

"So there you have it. All my deep, dark secrets."

Somehow, Cassie doubted that very much. "What are you going to do now?"

"Find another job, I guess. Keep looking for the killer. He's out there somewhere. And if I don't find him, he'll kill again. Maybe he already has." Jack's gaze left the street then and met hers. "What about you? What are you going to do?"

She fiddled with the gossamer skirt of her dress. "I don't know. I never thought I'd come back to Manville, but…here I am."

"You don't have to stay, you know."

"There's no reason for me to go back to Houston now, except to get Sam. Besides, I have a house here. And I could probably go back to teaching if I want to."

"Is that what you want?"

"I…don't know."

Jack was silent for a moment, then he said, "You told me once you'd always dreamed of being an artist, but you gave it up to take care of your mother. There's nothing holding you back now. Why not give it a try?"

"Because I don't have any talent," she said flatly.

"Now you're being modest."

"No, I'm not." She shoved back a strand of limp hair. "I'm being realistic. I always told myself that under different circumstances, I could have done exactly what Celeste did. I could have pursued my dreams, too. But you know what? Being an artist was just a pipe dream, and it's time I admit that. It's time to let go of that particular fantasy." And she did so with hardly more than a prickle of regret.

"Well," Jack said. "There are a lot of other things you could do. Why not try something different?"

"Like what?"

"I've been thinking about opening my own P.I. firm. I might be looking for a partner. Are you interested?"

Cassie's pulse leaped with sudden excitement. Was she *interested?* Was she *interested?* Oh, she was interested all right, but she tried not to jump at the offer. She didn't want to be too hasty here. Jack had lied to her, after all. Of course, she'd lied to him, too, so maybe that made them even. "I don't know the first thing about detective work."

He dismissed her concern. "You could learn. It's not like we'd be opening our doors overnight. It could take months or even years to get this thing off the ground. In the meantime, you could take some classes. You and Sam could even stay with me until…you know…you find your own place."

And if she played her cards right, that search

could take a good long while, Cassie thought. "Are you sure you want to make an offer like that? You've only known me for a couple days. For all you know, I could turn out to be some psycho."

"Or you could turn out to be the most wonderful woman I've ever met," he murmured.

Her heart started to pound in earnest. When she turned to stare at him, he smiled. And Cassie was lost.

"You did say you wanted an adventure, didn't you?" he murmured.

"Yes, I guess I did."

He smiled. "The way I see it, we've got some pretty interesting chemistry. Why not see where it takes us?"

Why not, indeed? "But starting a business together…surely there's someone else you know who's more qualified—"

"There's no one else."

Something in his voice, that look in his eyes, sent one of those little shudders through Cassie.

He leaned over and pressed his shoulder against hers. "What do you say? Partners?"

Cassie drew a long breath. "Partners." She held out her hand. He took it and lifted it to his mouth, skimming his lips across her knuckles. Cassie shivered in anticipation.

A partnership with Jack Fury? What was she thinking?

Her, a P.I.? No way she could pull that off.

But, boy, would she ever have fun trying!

And along the way, she just might find herself head over heels in love with the most exciting man she'd ever met.

It was worth a shot, wasn't it?

* * * * *

Look for the next exciting story in
Amanda Stevens's
MATCHMAKERS UNDERCOVER *series,*
JUST PAST MIDNIGHT
Available wherever Harlequin books are sold.

Like a phantom in the night comes
a new promotion from

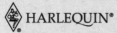 HARLEQUIN®

INTRIGUE®

GOTHIC ROMANCE

Beginning in August 2004, we offer you
a classic blend of chilling suspense and
electrifying romance, starting with….

A DANGEROUS INHERITANCE
LEONA KARR

And don't miss a spine-tingling Eclipse tale each month!

September 2004
MIDNIGHT ISLAND SANCTUARY
SUSAN PETERSON

October 2004
THE LEGACY OF CROFT CASTLE
JEAN BARRETT

November 2004
THE MAN FROM FALCON RIDGE
RITA HERRON

December 2004
EDEN'S SHADOW
JENNA RYAN

Available wherever Harlequin books are sold.
www.eHarlequin.com

HIECLIPSE

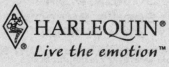

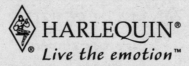

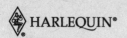

HARLEQUIN®

INTRIGUE®

and

B.J. DANIELS

invite you to join us for a trip to...

McCalls' Montana

Their land stretched for miles across
the Big Sky state...all of it hard earned—
none of it negotiable. Could family ties
withstand the weight of lasting legacy?

Starting in September 2004 look for:

THE COWGIRL
IN QUESTION

and

COWBOY ACCOMPLICE

**More books to follow
in the coming months.**

Available wherever Harlequin books are sold.

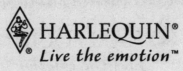

HARLEQUIN®
Live the emotion™

www.eHarlequin.com

HIMCCM

Dear Harlequin Intrigue Reader,

To chase away those end-of-summer blues, we have an explosive lineup that's guaranteed to please!

Joanna Wayne leaves goosebumps with *A Father's Duty*, the third book in NEW ORLEANS CONFIDENTIAL. In this riveting conclusion, murder, mayhem…and mystique are unleashed in the Big Easy. And that's just the beginning! *Unauthorized Passion*, which marks the beginning of Amanda Stevens's new action-packed miniseries, MATCHMAKERS UNDERGROUND, features a lethally sexy lawman who takes a beautiful imposter into his protective custody. Look for *Just Past Midnight* by Ms. Stevens from Harlequin Books next month at your favorite retail outlet.

Danger and discord sweep through Antelope Flats when B.J. Daniels launches her western series, McCALLS' MONTANA. Will the town ever be the same after a fiery showdown between a man on a mission and *The Cowgirl in Question*? Next up, the second book in ECLIPSE, our new gothic-inspired promotion. *Midnight Island Sanctuary* by Susan Peterson—a spine-tingling "gaslight" mystery set in a remote coastal town—will pull you into a chilling riptide.

To wrap up this month's thrilling lineup, Amy J. Fetzer returns to Harlequin Intrigue to unravel a sinister black-market baby ring mystery in *Undercover Marriage*. And, finally, don't miss *The Stolen Bride* by Jacqueline Diamond— an edge-of-your-seat reunion romance about an amnesiac bride-in-jeopardy who is about to get a crash course in true love.

Enjoy!

Denise O'Sullivan
Senior Editor
Harlequin Intrigue

She was just a job....

And if he had any sense, he'd keep their relationship on a purely professional basis. He had enough to worry about right now. Like who was out to get Celeste.

Someone had blown up that boat, trashed the beach house, and the suspect might well be the person he'd seen the other night trying to break into her hotel suite. The perp appeared to be getting bolder and more desperate by the day, and Jack knew from experience that desperation was a very dangerous commodity.

Romance would only complicate matters. Except a woman like Celeste didn't come along every day....